THE ADVENTURES OF FIRESKY

Savior Publishing

THE ADVENTURES OF FIRESKY

RAVEN OF THE NILE

by

XAVIER D WAYE

Savior Publishing

Books may be purchased in quantity and/or special sales by
contacting the publisher, Savior Publishing, LLC, at PO Box
250708, Atlanta, Georgia 30325; Telephone 762-585-5198, by
faxing 404-963-0900 or by email at saviorpublishing@gmail.com

Published by: Savior Publishing, LLC, Atlanta, Georgia
Interior Design by: Dr. Marjorie Waye
Cover Design by: German Creative
Editing by: Alberta Rainey
ISBN: 978-0-9861542-1-8

10 9 8 7 6 5 4 3 2

1.Historical-Fiction 2. Realistic-Fiction. 3. Adventure-Fiction 4.
Legend-Fiction
Printed in the U.S.A.

THE ADVENTURES OF FIRESKY
RAVEN OF THE NILE

CONTENTS

*To my fellow writer
my Great Grandmother*

1

THE TRIP OF A LIFETIME

My eyes flew open from what could be called a night of rest. I am far too excited, because today is the day. Today, my family and I leave for Egypt. After five years of hearing my Dad talk about how badly he wanted to take my brother and me to see where he grew up. Five years of stories, that started with, "When I was a Kid I lived in the Valley of the Kings..." and ended with "I can't wait to show you how you are related to King Tut."

As I lay here under my SpongeBob Square pants covers in Fifty Lakes, Minnesota, I think of what it will be like in Egypt. I know Egypt will be warmer than Minnesota, because outside my window all I see is white, white, white snow. I see more snow on my window than I see the glimmer of light from the moon through the sliver of window not covered with snow.

I turn my head to my right and look at my Avengers alarm clock that reads: Friday, February 19, 2016, 6:18 am. It is the last day of school before a weeklong winter break. Any other day Mom would have to drag me out of bed, but today I am wide-awake with so much excitement I could barely sleep.

Will Egypt have mounds of sands that we will hike through, like early American settlers? Will it be so windy that the sand will make it nearly impossible to see in front of our faces? Will we have to wear a kufiyah over our heads and a linen tunic to protect us from the extreme heat? What about sandals on our feet to keep our feet from burning up in the sand? I have read so much about Ancient Egypt in anticipation of this trip that I may have a slightly exaggerated image of modern-day Egypt. Either way, I know traveling to Egypt will likely be the most memorable trip of my lifetime. My Dad says we are related to King Tutankhamun, but with all of the books I have read and the family tree I created back in the fourth grade on the Great Kings of Ancient Egypt I never saw where he had kids.

From the hallway, I hear my Mom call, "Theo, it's Time to Wake Up!"

"Mom, I'm awake!"

"Really! Are you Sick?" Mom says.

"No! Today – Is - The - Day!" I yell back my words in a staccato fashion.

I hear my Dad squeal from his bathroom, followed by garbled unrecognizable words that I assume is because he is brushing his teeth. A few seconds later, I hear my Dad say; "It's time to Go Home!"

The excitement in my house is so hot; we could probably melt all of the snow around our house on our way out of the door.

I make my way to the bathroom to look at myself in the mirror, and to be sure that this day has indeed come. As I look up in the mirror, my eyes resemble the sleepless cat on the old Nickelodeon Cartoon Cat-Dog when his eyes were bloodshot from staying awake for a week because Dog wanted to win a contest where they had to stay awake longer than anyone else. I did not care; I figured I would sleep on the 15-hour flight from St Paul, Minnesota to Luxor, Egypt. My floppy brown hair and big hazel eyes set too deep in my round face looked brighter than usual, considering I did not have to get dragged out of bed this morning. I made quick time brushing my teeth, washing my face, and brushing my hair trying not to picture myself in Egypt tomorrow morning doing the same things. I dress in my uniform for St Paul preparatory school and know that this last day of 5th grade leading into winter break will take FOREVER.

My brother, Rudy is in the 7th grade, and he is more excited than me. He beat me downstairs for breakfast this morning. My mom should probably take a picture of this because other than Christmas this is likely the only day of the year we beat her to breakfast.

"Ok Gang, let's go over the plans for today," my dad says.

Rudy and I sit up in our seats hoping Dad will surprise us by telling us we don't have to go to school today. But to our disappointment, Dad tells us that our flight leaves after we get out of school.

Dad tells us our schedules, hazel eyes bright and filled with excitement saying," Ok, so our flight leaves at 7 pm from St Paul International Airport. Mom, will meet you both in front St Paul Prep at 2:30 pm. Please do not move slowly today!", Dad says sternly while piercing his eyes at Rudy, more than me.

My brother Rudy, although almost six feet tall with long wiry legs, moves at a glacial pace everywhere he goes. He can technically take one-step for every two steps of a normal person, yet chooses to move slowly everywhere he goes. He drives my Mom crazy. Today, however, is the most excited I have seen Rudy, I don't believe he will waste any time getting to the car because it means we're that much closer to Egypt.

Dad continued to share our schedule saying, "After we pick you both up, we will head straight to the Airport which will take about 2 ½ hours. Mom and I will pack up the car with our luggage, then we will fly out of St Paul Airport and travel to Egypt over 15 hours." Dad's energy was seeping through his dark olive skin as he described our trip, I thought his wavy buzz cut hair was going to stand up on his head.

Dad continued, "After we arrive in Egypt we will rest to adjust to the time change and tomorrow we are scheduled to take a tour of, the City of Luxor, The Valley of the Kings to include Karnack, Temple Luxor, Ancient Thebes, along with a boat ride along the Nile. This will be the trip of a lifetime; I promise."

As Dad described our tour, I found myself day-dreaming about what I can expect. I looked out of the kitchen window, staring at the snow imagining the sand cascading the hills of Luxor, and as I looked at the horizon just past the sand in the immense heat, I could see the crest of the temples at Karnack. Apparently, I daydreamed so long, that my Mom had to call me three times and smack me on the head to pull me out of my daydream.

Mom called out to Rudy and me telling us it was time to leave for school. I grabbed my backpack and another muffin from the stove and headed for the garage door. Leaving for school was a ritualistic nightmare during winter. I know this same ritual occurred in every home in Minnesota because as all students arrived at St Paul Prep, we all looked like stuffed teddy bears. I put on my black gloves, scarf, black bib snow pants, and black and lime hooded puffer jacket along with my favorite Merrill grey and lime snow boots. My boots looked more like old school Adidas converse than snow boots did. I figured if I have to wear this bear suit, I might as well have some style. As if putting on all of the snow gear, assuring I would not feel the hint of cold, was not enough I topped off my bear suit with a black Cabela's face mask. If it weren't for the fact that everyone in school wore a face mask during the winter months, my dark olive skin in that black mask would make me a great candidate for a bank robber.

Finally, after 10 minutes of converting to an Eskimo, we pile into Mom's 2013 Cadillac Escalade truck as the garage door creeks open. Mom eases out onto the freshly paved driveway, compliments of our neighbor's son Charlie, who earns a whopping $10.00 per day for shoveling five neighbor's driveways each morning at 5 am. Charlie, who is 15 years old, has been saving for his car that he won't buy until he turns 16 next year. I can't knock the kids hustle, although I couldn't do it for $50.00 per week, just doesn't seem worth it to me.

Mom drives Rudy and me to school on the clean streets of Fifty Lakes, compliments of the city shovel machines. After five minutes, we arrive at St Paul prep and peel ourselves out of the truck. I look around and see the sea of stuffed bear students making their way to the front door of the school so we can all peel out of our bear or Eskimo snow gear. St Paul preparatory school is nothing if it is not prepared for receiving the snow gear from 500 students. In the past 5 years, the school installed a rotating closet just inside the front door. Every day we enter the school front doors, turn right into what looks like the front office but instead is attended by three teachers who take our snow gear and snow boots and put them in a revolving cubby that looks like mini lockers on a dry cleaner's conveyor belt. Each time the attendant takes our gear, they give us a ticket that resembles a raffle ticket and then presses a button to move to the next cubby and accept the next guy's snow gear. The process is ingenious because it allows us to move freely in the climate-controlled hallways and classrooms without the concerns of slipping and sliding from some guy's residual snow or ice that accidentally fell off their snows shoes.

I walk into Mrs. Goddess's fifth-grade class and take my seat next to Princess Simpson, the nicest most annoying girl in the class. She is very nice to me, too nice to me, always asking me about what I am doing, how is my class going, what do I have planned for the break? If I didn't know any better, I would think she was a spy for some secret agency. As I sit down, I ready myself for the inquisition, and she does not disappoint.

Princess swings her shoulder-length blond hair over her shoulder, looks longingly at me with her light blue eyes, inhales and says, "Theo, what do you have planned for the Winter Break? My family and I are going up to Canada for an ice-fishing trip. We will be staying in a hotel called the igloo, even though it is not actually an igloo. It's going to be Super Cool," Princess says.

Although I could fill the whole class time with my expectations and excitement surrounding my family trip to Egypt, I cannot take the extra inquisition she will grill me with if I tell her all about Egypt. I say, "My family and I are going on a trip back to my Dad's hometown, for the break." I didn't lie to her I simply did not embellish about my trip to Egypt.

The day dragged on from subject to subject, with the occasional break for lunch and surprise ice cream hand out after lunch commemorating our last day before winter break. Finally, 2:30 arrived, and the bell rang in a way that spoke to me. It seemed to be telling me that after this day my life would change.

I gathered my backpack and pulled out my snow gear ticket so that I would waste no time getting out to mom's truck. I met Rudy at the snow gear office; we looked at each other his brown eyes to my hazel with flecks of glee that seemingly radiated from our skin because of our excitement. As soon as we dressed, we darted for the door, scanning the rows of vehicles looking for Mom's gold escalade. Rudy spotted it first and took off running. I ran after him feeling like I was wobbling in my Bear/Eskimo suit. I saw Mom twirling her long sandy brown hair as she always did when she was anxious or excited. As we grew closer to the truck, I could see Mom's brown eyes fixed on the rear-view mirror transfixed in a gaze I saw far too often, the glare of daydreaming, undoubtedly about the anticipation of traveling to Egypt. Even though my mom had lived there when she was a kid, she appeared to be just as excited as Rudy and me about seeing Egypt. Mom escaped her daydream as we approached the car, put the key in the ignition, and started the Cadillac.

"I dropped your father off at the drug store to get some motion sickness pills so we will pick him up on our way to the airport," Mom said.

About 3 minutes later, we arrive at Walgreens to pick up dad who, standing outside of the store, had the same dazed look that Mom had while she was awaiting Rudy and me. Mom had to call to Dad three times to break him from his daydream. As Dad climbed into the car, I asked him what was wrong with him.

He grinned and said, "I can't help visualizing what home is like now. It's been more than 15 years since I was in Egypt and I almost want to cry when I think back on the days at my home."

"I believe you boys will have the adventure of a lifetime," Dad said.

"Dad, I feel it in the pit of my stomach, we are in for an amazing journey," I said as we traveled down US-10.

The sides of the highway looked like black and white mounds of snow, which looked like Oreo cookies and Vanilla Bean ice cream mixed up in a blender at a slow speed. I believe the lack of sleep combined with my excitement put me to sleep during the 2-1/2-hour drive to the airport.

We arrived at the airport, checked into our flight, checked our luggage, and made haste down the airport corridor to our gate. I do not believe I saw anyone's faces while traveling through the airport. As I took each step toward my gate, I felt the twisting in my stomach that things were about to change, but I was unable to say what the change would be.

I sat next to Dad at the gate, and I looked at him as if to study his face. His dark olive skin, round face, flushed puffy cheeks, and creased brow, which seemed to make his hazel eyes set deeper into his face was all focused on one thing, a daydream or distant thought, presumably about going home, his original home Egypt.

"Dad, are you alright?" I asked.

"Yes, son! I am just excited about going home," Dad said with a comforting smile.

"Is there anything I need to know before we get there?" I said, thinking in the back of my mind anything I need to know outside of the 5,000 times he told us the stories about his home.

"Son, your mom and I want this trip to be an amazing experience for you and your brother. I hope that you get some history about your family and finally get to see proof of Raven and Firesky." Dad explained

Just as Dad finished making his statement to me, we hear the disembodied voice of a woman over the intercom saying, "Would

Abraham and Tangela Bishara, please come to the attendance desks."

Both Dad and Mom rose to walk over to the attendant's desk, while I looked out of the window thinking back on the thousands of times I heard Dad's stories. I never recalled him telling me about anyone named Raven or Firesky. My eyes flickered from side to side recollecting all of the details in the stories. I remembered hearing him telling Rudy and me that we're related to King Tut. I recalled hearing about his home near the Valley of the Kings. I remembered hearing about his parents, his family, and his friends. I remember listening intently to his stories about the magic of Egypt, about the Kingdoms of the 18th century, the villages that supported the kingdom, and a lady named Imani. I could not recall anyone named Raven or Firesky.

I looked over at Rudy, who was playing a game on his iPhone.

"Hey Rudy, do you remember anyone in Dads Egypt stories named Raven or Firesky?" I asked.

"Who are they?" Rudy responded in an irritated voice, still playing his game.

"I don't know, Dad just said he hopes we get a chance to find out more about Raven and Firesky while we are in Egypt, but I don't remember him ever telling us about these people," I said to Rudy.

Rudy looked away from his game turned his head toward me and glared out the window. After a few seconds, Rudy looked at me intently and said, "I remember one story about Dad's uncle who would talk to him about a child named fire something who saved a girl who was part of the royal court during King Tut's time."

Rudy looked up to see that Mom and Dad were returning to our seats and stopped talking when Dad said we were upgraded to business class on our flight because he had so many points on his American Express credit card. This would give us more space on the flight of 15 hours and more food for the trip. A great start for the trip of a lifetime. In the back of my head, I wanted to hear the rest of the story from Rudy but decided to wait until we were settled in our seats to ask more questions.

We boarded the KLM Boeing 777 flight that would take us from Minneapolis to Amsterdam and then from Amsterdam to Luxor, Egypt. As we walked into business class I saw that the seats looked like little cubbies. Each row of seats had four seats, one at each window and two in the middle of the plane. The seats looked similar to the Guppy Bubbler ride at Nickelodeon Universe amusement park at The Mall of America®. They were curved like half of a teacup with a seat that had a cushion and faced a television screen. The two seats in the middle of the aisle looked like two teacups connected to each other both with seats and seat cushions each facing a television screens. Although the teacup seats were connected, they appeared to have their own private spaces. The legroom for all of the seats looked like enough room for my friend Aaron's dad who is 6'7" tall.

As we made our way to our seats I sat in one of the seats in the middle of business class. Dad sat in the teacup seat next to me, while Rudy sat in the window seat next to Dad and Mom in the window seat next to me. I leaned forward in my seat to look at Dad whose head appeared hidden behind a console of gadgets and buttons that resembled a scene from Star Trek® when Captain Kirk was in his seat and at his head and hands were buttons and gadgets to control the Enterprise. Dad caught a glimpse of my face and leaned toward me with a frown on his brow as if to ask without words if I was all right.

"Dad, these seats don't look like they were designed for us to talk," I said.

Dad answered with his reassuring grin, "Son, we have a week to talk, let's just enjoy the flight and try to get some much-needed sleep before we get to Egypt because I suspect we will not be sleeping too much in Egypt."

Dad was right, but I was unclear about what to expect, now that I understood I actually didn't know the full story about our history. Who was this Raven and Firesky? What did they have to do with King Tut or me? How did I miss the details of the story Rudy started to tell me about in the Airport? Instead of feeling like I was ready to explore our history once we arrived in Egypt, I now felt like I would hear a new story, a story I only knew bits and pieces about all my life.

As the plane took off for Amsterdam, the flight attendant, a tall lengthy Asian woman with short and highlighted brown and black hair, began instructing us passengers on what to expect of the Boeing 777 airplane, on the safety guidelines should the plane drop from the sky and land in the ocean. I heard half of her speech, but the rumble of the takeoff made my eyelids heavier and heavier until I could hold them open no more and I fell off into a deep sleep. It turned out the teacup seats were perfect for sleeping. I drifted off to sleep with images of a boy and a girl in Egypt named Firesky and Raven somehow tied to King Tut.

CHAPTER TWO

ANOTHER STORY THAT THEY NEVER WANTED TOLD

I woke up to the disembodied voice on the intercom from the pilot flying our plane. The pilot explained that we were approaching Amsterdam International Airport where the local time was 6:00 am, and the local temperature was 5 degrees Celsius/41 degrees Fahrenheit. I realized as I fought to open my eyes that we had flew 8 hours, and I slept the entire way. I hadn't realized my excitement made me so exhausted, but now that my brain was waking up I began to get more and more excited.

I glanced over at my Mom's window to see the sky over Amsterdam was a mix of dark blue and orange which meant the sun was just below the horizon. I thought to myself, how awesome it would be to see the sunrise in another country; one of the first experiences in this trip of a lifetime.

A few minutes later, the plane touched down on the tarmac of the Amsterdam International Airport. The lights of the cabin turned on, and I felt the touch of my mother's hand on my arm. I turned to my Mom who looked refreshed from a full night of undisturbed sleep. Her brown eyes were clear and bright and her hair had been pulled back into a ponytail. She smiled a wide, bright smile at me, showing her perfect white teeth, and said; "Theo, did you get some rest, you were looking a bit tired before we left?"

The image of the old cat-dog episode popped back into my head, and I thought I hope I did not look that bad. I responded to Mom saying," I had a great sleep Mom, but I think this may be the last good sleep I get until we get back home."

Mom and I both laughed and looked over at Dad and Rudy who appeared to be laughing at their own similar joke.

We gathered our belongings, got off the airplane, and walked into the Amsterdam International Airport terminal. As we entered the terminal, it reminded me of The Mall of America® back in Minnesota minus the amusement park in the middle of the mall. The terminal was filled with areas for shopping, food, clothes, and jewelry, with a candy shop I caught from the corner of my eye. As I looked down the corridor from our gate, it looked like a street with direction signs to tell you which hall or street you were on or headed to inside the airport. The stores looked like glass boxes or attached Lego® blocks with the illuminated store names behind the glass boxes. The first store I saw was the Wonder Woman® store. From outside the window, I could see various souvenirs and trinkets available. Since our flight was leaving from the same terminal 9 where we arrived, Mom decided to walk around to the Amsterdam shops. I was not completely awake so Dad and I decided to sit in the comfortable chairs of the waiting area of terminal 9.

"Dad, can you tell me who Firesky was?" I asked without giving my dad a chance to sit down.

"Theo, Firesky was a boy who decided to take his future and the future of his family into his own hands," Dad said in answer to my question. He continued, "Firesky, was the brother, or adopted brother, as he would discover of Raven the daughter of King Tutankhamun."

"Dad, how is this possible?" I responded, dumbfounded at his words. "King Tutankhamun was married to his sister, and they had two stillborn children, there were no reports of any other biological children belonging to King Tutankhamun in any book I read," I replied emphatically.

"Theo, I understand the history currently written in the history books of Ancient Egypt. However, there is another story that the Ancient Egyptians never wanted to be told, the story of the love affair between a girl of status in a neighboring community of ancient Thebes and

King Tutankhamun. My brother knows the story in detail, much better than me. I know the bits and pieces of the stories he would tell when I was a child. He is the keeper of the story as it is passed down from generation to generation typically to the oldest boy." Dad explained.

"Why didn't you ever tell me the whole story? I mean with Firesky and Raven? "I asked.

"Theo, I always told you the stories with Firesky and Raven as a bedtime story. The reason you didn't remember Firesky and Raven is because you fell off to sleep before I made it to that part of the story." Dad expressed with a slight chuckle.

In my head I said, that makes a lot of sense. But why would he elect to share this important detail about my family history in a bedtime story? I mean, Really!!! Was that the only time he could talk about it. "Will we be able to talk with Uncle Aaron about the details of the story when we get to Egypt?" I asked Dad with expectant hope in my voice.

Dad nodded his head yes and said, "Son, that is what prompted this trip Aaron called me one day and told me I needed to bring you boys to Egypt as soon as possible as he finally put all of the pieces of our family history together. It was the perfect motivation to live my dream of taking you to see my home."

Now I was more intrigued by what awaited us in Egypt. Was there some major artifact or archeological discovery to be revealed to the world after our visit? Were we going to be crowned as the new royal family of Egypt? Maybe we are walking into a trap, and the Egyptian government wanted all family link to King Tutankhamun captured or killed to keep us from ever claiming to be royalty. Obviously, I have watched far too many episodes of the Twilight Zone on TV Land®.

I stared out the window of the terminal 9 waiting area watching planes land and take off from the tarmac. As I stared out of the window, I wondered how old Firesky was when he took his future and the future of his family into his own hands. If he was a kid, I wondered how he could have done anything on his own. Children in ancient Egypt were not empowered to do anything without their parents or overseers. It was hard to imagine a child doing anything that could change the future for anyone in ancient Egypt.

Mom called out to me, pulling me out of my daydream, to let me know it was time to board the plane for Luxor, Egypt. I looked up at my Mom and noticed she had three shopping bags. "Mom, what's in the bags," I asked.

Mom looked at me as if she ate a canary, I suppose because she did not want to be noticed by Dad. Dad was always saying mom shopped more than she breathed and we did not have room for one more thing on this trip. Mom, said she bought some lotion and perfume because she remembered she left it at the house as they were packing up the car. My Dad looked at her as she was explaining her shopping bags, and pressed his lips into a hard line, and arched his eyebrows but did not say anything to mom. As we boarded the airplane I noticed Mom's shoulder relaxed; I guess because Dad did not say anything about her new purchases. I whispered to Mom as we stopped at the door before to boarding, "It's because we are on vacation!" Mom turned her head slightly and smiled at me.

We boarded the airplane and headed to our business class teacup seats, as the same airplane that flew us to Amsterdam would take us into Luxor, Egypt. Mom and I switched seats so that I could sit by the window on this leg of the trip. The thought of being able to see us arrive in Egypt was exhilarating. I sat in the window teacup seat and these four hours would be far too exciting for me to fall asleep, I thought.

The flight attendant was now a woman of Egyptian descent. She had dark olive skin with her dark brown hair pulled up into a neat bun. She wore glasses and had a nice smile although she also looked very stern. She looked like my third-grade teacher Mrs. Parker who always appeared mad in the morning but mellowed out by lunchtime. We never seemed to get along in the mornings, so I never asked questions until after lunchtime.

As the plane taxied down the tarmac, the flight attendant shared all of the safety guidelines once again. Once again, the rumble of the airplane readying to take off seemed to make my eyelids heavy once more. The next thing I knew, my mom was calling out to me to tell me we were about to land. I woke up with a jolt thinking I missed the view from the plane of Egypt.

I looked out the window and to my delight found that we were close enough to see our descent but still high enough to see the layout of the land. Amazed, I looked down and saw mountainous regions that resembled branches of veins throughout the human body. The mountains appeared to interrupt the vast sandy plains of land, which even from the airplane looked to be never-ending. I saw a patchwork of green squares of land, which identified areas where people lived and were long ago uninhabited oasis among the sand. The sandy plains were expansive with random plots of palm trees and grass.

As the plane descended, the history of the land came into better view. I saw the Temple of Karnack. The monument built more than 2,000 years ago was easily identified by the dual Obelisks 29 meters in heights, which is almost ten stories high. The Obelisks are located in the Precinct of Amun Re at the opening of the Festival Hall of Thutmose III, next to the temple of Taharka next to the sacred lake. I easily identified the multiple sections of the temple with the primary areas sectioned off by what looked like rectangle walls of a large sand castle from the airplane. I was spellbound looking at how close the Nile River was to the Temple and remembered that the Nile was the primary transportation for products in an out of the area.

Although the ruins of the great Temple of Karnack, which takes up more than 200 acres, have been distressed over time, it is amazing to see how my studies of Ancient Egypt helped me to identify the vastness and the majesty of the Valley of the Kings. However, when I compared the images I saw in the books I read about Ancient Egypt I felt like I see a brand-new picture of Egypt as my research paled in comparison to the real thing.

As we grew closer to the city of Luxor, I tried to look back and soak up the images of The Temple of Karnack, but as the temple faded from my view I saw the Temple of Luxor. This temple that appeared to sit in the heart of modern-day Luxor Egypt. At the edge of the temple was a road with what looked like five or six lanes of traffic, which curved around the front of the temple. The temple appeared to be an elaborate maze from the airplane. As we descended closer to the ground, I could see the numerous columns of towers that looked like a massive design of dominos designed and ready to be toppled. The distance from the roadway in front of the monument to the rear of the temple looked like more than four or five city blocks. Similar to the Temple at Karnack the structure looked like a massive sand castle because of the sand, looking at it from the airplane. The Luxor Temple looked out of place, but I guess this is where ancient and modern Egyptian history meet.

I saw the airplane cross over onto the Luxor International Airport tarmac as the land under the plane changed from green land to concrete. I looked up and saw the airport terminal ahead of the plane moving closer and closer. The closer we came to the terminal the more excited I became. The greater the feeling that something amazing was about to happen. I was momentarily paralyzed by my excitement when I felt the bump of the airplane tires make contact with the Luxor International Airport Tarmac. The touchdown was followed by the sound of a windstorm as the flaps on the airplane wings flipped up to slow down the plane. Soon we were at the terminal gates packing up our carry-on luggage and de-boarding the plane. The moment my foot crossed the threshold into the Luxor International Terminal, I felt it. I felt the pull of change, the pull of monumental changes to the life I currently know, and I believed I was ready for it. I was ready to transcend time, give or take 2,000 years, and come face to face with a boy named Firesky and a girl named Raven.

CHAPTER THREE

NOT IN ANY HISTORY BOOK I HAVE EVER READ

I remember dad telling us we would begin our tour tomorrow after we adjusted to the time change, but it seemed Uncle Aaron had a GPS tracker on us. Ten steps into the Luxor International Airport my Dad's cell phone rang. I watched my dad's face turn from happy to distress in a matter of seconds. Dad hung up the phone and turned to Mom.

"Abraham, what's wrong?" Mom asked in a concerned voice.

"Aaron said we have to go with him right now, or our entire family legacy may be gone forever. He is waiting for us outside. He also said that Theo must be the key!" My dad said turning to look at me.

"What, why me, I don't understand," I answered stumbling over my words.

"Son, I don't think it's anything bad, but somehow you are the key to the mystery," Dad said as assuring as he could.

No matter what Dad could tell me or how comforting he tried to be, I was freaking out. I just came to see the sights, soak up the history, not to be an ancient Egyptian sacrifice to bring back some 2000-year-old mummy or something. I wanted to learn my history, but not as part of it. I enjoy learning my history in anonymity.

I took a deep breath and hoped I did not look as freaked out as I felt. We walked through the terminal, and I did not see one person we passed, I solely focused on any possible reason I am the key to anything. I felt the occasional pat on the shoulders and back from Mom, but otherwise transfixed on the words, Theo is the

Key!

We retrieved our bags from baggage claim, and as we approached the doorway to leave the Luxor International Airport, I noticed the time was 11:55 am, and the temperature was 21 degrees Celcius or 70 degrees Fahrenheit. I stepped through the doors of the terminal and there standing by the doors of a cream-colored minivan stood a man that looked hauntingly like my dad. He stood about six feet tall with a buzz cut hairstyle, dark olive skin, deep-set eyes that were hazel colored like my dad. My Dad grabbed my uncle Aaron in a bear hug, and I noticed that Aaron, although he was tall, he was much skinnier than my dad. Uncle Aaron and my dad stood clutching each other's arms at their elbows and looked at each other with genuine love for one another, after a few seconds they hugged each other again. My mom broke up the bothers so that she could greet my uncle. Mom hugged him and then grabbed Rudy to hug Aaron first and then Aaron grabbed me with his long right arm and pulled me into a group hug with Rudy. My Dad asked Uncle Aaron, "What's the emergency." Then Aaron separated from Rudy and me.

"Abraham, we found another compartment in the box with a message that speaks of a history that can only be endured through the innocence of a child. The passage of the box has always been to the first-born son of each generation however, there was a symbol embedded in the message that we translated that led straight to…" Aaron's voice trailed off as he turned and looked at me. With what felt like a huge baseball in my throat and a shaky voice I responded to Uncle Aarons silent stare with, "…straight to Me?"

I felt the eyes of Mom, Dad, and Rudy burrowing into my head, like sunlight through a magnifying glass. My whole body shook because I had no idea what this meant. I only learned about Firesky and Raven this morning, and now I am somehow the link between ancient and modern Egypt. This is Psycho, just yesterday, I was sleeping comfortably under my Spongebob Squarepants covers, now I am the link to the history of a dynasty? These types of things only happen in the movies, not to a boy from Fifty Lakes, Minnesota.

Uncle Aaron told us to get in the Minivan, and he would take us to a place where all would be revealed. We piled into the minivan onto the comfortable grey leather seats. I sat next to Dad and grabbed his hand to hold it for comfort. Dad seemed just as freaked out as I was. His hands were sweaty and were shaking, although it could have been my hands shaking enough for the both of us. I asked Dad, "What does this mean? Will I be able to go back home? What about you guys, does this mean we will be separated?"

Dad responded," Theo, why don't we just wait to hear what Aaron has to tell us. I am sure you will be just fine, and we will all go home at the end of the week."

Dad's response was not as confident or comforting as I wanted to hear. Mom's expression as she looked back at Dad from the middle row seat in the minivan was even less comforting. She looked so afraid for me, but until we understood the story, there was nothing any of us could do.

We arrived at the Valley of the Kings in what felt like an instant. I missed all of the history of the land we were driving past, in anticipation of the news Uncle Aaron had to share. I climbed out of the van onto the sandy soil that covered everything in sight and looked around at the crowds of people looking at the magnificence created thousands of years ago. I looked up to see the entrance to the tomb of Tutankhamun, my fear momentarily transformed to awe. I was here, here at the tomb of the boy king. I was here in the epicenter of the legacy and majesty of many of the great pharaohs of ancient Egypt.

Uncle Aaron came around the driver's side of the van and motioned for us to enter the tomb of King Tutankhamun. The entrance to the tomb was flanked by triangle walls which brought back images of the 1923 discovery. I remember seeing the pictures of the original discovery of the tomb back in 1923 that looked like a small rectangular opening flanked by these triangle walls. Today as

I walk through the opening, I understand that the doorway today was much larger than what appeared in the old pictures. The door was about 6 feet tall; I remember my uncle had to duck to enter the doorway. As we walked through the doorway, there was a stairway leading down into the tomb. The stairway was dimly lit by what looked like candles on the walls. The stairs felt like stone stairs covered with the grit of sand. The air felt thick and humid like a summers day in the deep south but with 70 degrees outside. I was comfortable and terrified at the same time.

When we started down the stairs to the tomb, I glanced back up the stairs and noticed there were no visitors behind us. I wondered if it was a coincidence and kept walking down the stairs. We entered the antechamber of the tomb to see the coarseness of the sand colored walls. I walked around the wall feeling the bare unpainted chamber. Uncle Aaron stood at the door looking back for incoming visitors. As I approached the back-wall Uncle Aaron walked behind me and grabbed my left hand. Rudy was beside me immediately and reached out to Uncle Aaron to protect me from any immediate danger. Dad who had examined the walls of the antechamber from the opposite direction than I started turning around and looked and said, "Aaron what are you doing?"

Aaron said nothing and took my hand to a spot on the back wall of the antechamber. It was about two feet from the wall that was the entrance to the king's burial chamber. Again, my Dad called out to Aaron asking him, "Aaron what are you doing with Theo." Again, Uncle Aaron ignored my dad and instead pressed my hand into the spot. The spot was softer than the rest of the wall, and with the pressure from both Aaron and myself, the spot went into the wall about the depth of my elbow. A few seconds later we heard the rumble of the wall moving into a doorway that seemed to appear from nowhere. A piece of the rock wall, about three feet wide and five feet high moved to the right behind the wall of the antechamber. The movement of the doorway seemed to release some pressure, and a billow of sand appeared. As the sand settled Uncle Aaron crossed the threshold of this new doorway and a few moments later light appeared beyond the doorway showing a small room. Without thinking, I walked into the room and heard my mom gasp and say, "Theo Wait!" I turned to look back at mom, who was standing outside of the doorway inspecting it to see if it was a trap. Finally, my dad took her by the arm and led her into the room after Rudy stepped beyond the door. Uncle Aaron walked over to the magical door and pressed something else, and the doorway closed.

My Dad stood and looked at Aaron in a way I had never seen before. Dad looked so angry I think I saw steam coming from his head.

"Aaron, what's with all the theatrics, you brought my family here just to trap us in a room and what…?" Dad said.

"Abraham, about six months ago I found the extra compartment to the box and this message contained on a very old piece of linen paper. I took the paper to the Directors of Ancient History at Cairo University. They called me about two weeks later to meet with me privately. They met me at my house and informed me that the message contained details of this secret compartment and that the walls contained a message for the future of this legacy. The message told of a boy in the lineage who would be the link to preserve this message for all eternity. The lineage foretells of the first-born son of each generation being the protector of the secret up to our generation and then it changes," Uncle Aaron said fading off.

"Changes to What?" I yelled out accidentally.

"Changes to You, and then the message says the passing stops." Uncle Aaron said in a confused tone.

"I am so confused Uncle Aaron, what secret, passing what, what box? Is this connected to Firesky and Raven? Please tell me, tell me the full story." I said now shaking from my growing fear.

In the small room, I felt a breeze of air from the door, which I suspected kept the room cool enough for us to sit and hear this great secret, this pendulum of destiny I am going to have to carry. There were two benches in the room, mom, dad, Rudy and I sat on one bench while Uncle Aaron fidgeted with the light. As Uncle Aaron was messing with the lights, he told us that very few people knew the story he was about to share and made us swear to a lifetime of secrecy to preserve our family line. We all swore because no one but my dad had a clue about what he was about to share. Just after we all swore, Uncle Aaron lit a match, touched it to the wall and the whole room lit up.

Now that we could see all of the walls in this small room behind the antechamber, I saw all of the hieroglyphics and drawing on the walls. Floor to ceiling details of someone's story, of life never revealed to the public. This was not in any history book I have ever read, not in anyone's tale of the life of King Tutankhamun. At one place on the left back wall from where we sat was a life-sized painting of King Tutankhamun in his infamous headdress. To the left and right sat children with one child larger than the other. A girl child with long black hair and hazel colored eyes.

Off to the right of Tutankhamun, I saw a woman with darker brown skin and long black hair reaching out to him from a hillside. Beside her looked to be an older man and woman dressed in royal linens and a younger boy who was not much older than me. The walls paintings also included a soldier who seemed to be holding a box of some kind.

After seeing the box on the wall, I slowly turned to Aaron who was watching me intently. "Is that the box you were talking about?" I hesitantly asked my uncle.

Aaron peered down at me, and without saying a word leaned down to the floor, picked up his back-pack opened it and pulled out the gold box. I looked at the box in Uncle Aaron's hands and immediately looked at the painting of the box on the cave wall. The boxes were the same! The gold-plated details on the box on the wall included intricate symbols surrounded by flowers. There were etchings of wheat stalks and other trees with fruits. There was an etching of a bird peering down on a crowd. Each of the details I saw on the box in Uncle Aaron's hands appeared on the box that the soldier was holding on the picture. Reality finally dawned on me that the box in Uncle Aaron's hands was over 2000 years old and close enough for me to touch. I looked up at Uncle Aaron as if to ask him, just with my eyes, can I touch it? Uncle Aaron through the same silent communication handed me the box.

The box was just a little heavy, like holding about four school math books. Each side of the boxes were delicately embellishment with frames of smooth gold. Each side looked like framed pictures and each frame contained a carving made with depth and texture. The pictures however had texture and depth to the etchings. The embellishments, on this box could not have been done as quickly as the tomb preparation for King Tutankhamun. It was obvious, this box was the work of a skilled craftsman or artist who took their time and created this gold masterpiece. Come to think of it, to paint this much detail on the walls of the cave someone had to have taken just as much time to create the cave drawings.

"Uncle Aaron, please tell me the story of this cave, this box, and where I fit in as the key, "I said giving way to my curiosity instead of my anxiety.

CHAPTER FOUR

A GIFT TO THE KING

When King Tutankhamun (pronounced "To-Tan-Common") was eleven, he had officially been King over Egypt for two years, although the kingdom was actually being ruled by his vizier AY (pronounced "I") and the priest of the kingdom. AY would spend time with Tutankhamun under the guise that he was teaching Tutankhamun how to be a true King and rule the land with respect and power. In truth, AY would give Tutankhamun tasks to do in the kingdom, none of which would help him to rule the kingdom nor learn how to be an effective leader. AY would appoint Tutankhamun to attend festivals and rituals to RA the Sun God, but again never to teach him how to lead or rule the kingdom. After a year, when Tutankhamun turned twelve, Egypt was attacked by an

Ethiopian army. In an attempt to protect King Tutankhamun AY appointed a faction of the military to surround Tutankhamun and Ankhesenamun (pronounced "An-K-Say-Na-Moon") at all times. The faction of the military included a young man thirteen years old named David. Over a period of four months, while the Egyptian and Ethiopian armies battled Tutankhamun and David became best friends.

As the battle ended between the Egyptian Army and the Ethiopian Army with the Egyptian army being the victor, AY decided to fortify Egypt by forging a relationship with all of the surrounding Egyptian communities. Having appointed Tutankhamun as the local Ambassador to each of the surrounding communities for the past twelve months, AY felt it necessary to dispatch Tutankhamun and the faction of the Egyptian Army on a monthly tour to each of the local villages surrounding Egypt. Each of the villages had their appointed government and leadership, which meant Tutankhamun would have to spend time with each of the leaders to determine what it would take to make them align with the Egyptian Kingdom to help fortify it.

If the Ethiopian Army returned and tried to kill the King before he and Ankhesenamun gave birth to an heir, AY decided to have Tutankhamun trained in advanced chariot racing, combat strategy, and hand to hand combat training. David was appointed as one of his military trainers, which pleased both David and Tutankhamun. After his training, Tutankhamun his caravan of military personnel, and supplies embarked on their monthly visits to the villages that surrounded the Kingdom. Although the kingdom controlled these regional villages they were too far to control on a day to day basis and therefore were left to govern themselves. The governance included what some would call local royalty with a royal family and other layers of leadership underneath the royal family.

Tutankhamun and his caravan had gone on three other visits to local villages before coming to a village called Khuhua. Khuhua was one of the largest villages outside of the Kingdom and had more than 10,000 people in the community.

The local royalty was a fair governor named Tuhar. Tuhar had a wife named Anai, and two children, the older child, a daughter named Imani, and a younger child named Steven. Tuhar had visited the Kingdom many times and knew King Akhenaten (pronounced "Ahk-Na-Ten") when he was alive.

Tutankhamun approached the home of Tuhar to much celebration and welcome. Tutankhamun hosted a grand ball the prior year in the City of Khuhua to celebrate their wheat harvest. So, the people in the villages were aware of and very happy with the relationship between their village and the Kingdom represented by Tutankhamun. As Tutankhamun approached Tuhar's home, he was pleased to see Tuhar was standing at the gate of his home with his wife on his right side, his daughter on his left side, and his son in front of his daughter awaiting their presence.

Tutankhamun dismounted from his chariot, and with David, his soldier and friend, at his side walked to the entrance of the gate to

Tuhar's home. "Greetings my great King Tutankhamun, thank you for gracing our village with your presence today. You and your caravan are welcome in my village. In anticipation of your arrival we have arranged for your accommodations in our home," Governor Tuhar said.

As Tuhar greeted Tutankhamun, David noticed that Tutankhamun could not stop looking at Imani, Tuhar's daughter. David had never noticed his friend looking so intently at a woman before. David had watched Tutankhamun and Ankhesenamun together, but never did he see Tutankhamun watch or even look at Ankhesenamun like he was looking Imani. He looked at Ankhesenamun with approval and admiration when she advanced in her academics or looked beautiful in a gown the kingdom designers made for her, but never with the look of intensity he was giving to Imani that day.

When David looked over at Imani, although she was stone faced, he could see the peak of a smile on her lips noticing the intense stare from Tutankhamun. After Governor Tuhar's introduction, Tutankhamun was able to gather himself and follow Governor Tuhar's family into their home. David was the only other person to accompany Tutankhamun into the home, as the remainder of the Caravan stayed outside and unpacked the gifts and packages they had brought from the Kingdom.

Tuhar asked his wife and children to retire to the back room to provide an opportunity for governor Tuhar to speak in private with King Tutankhamun. They spent the next hour talking about what had happened in the battle and the need to fortify all of the cities in an around the Kingdom. Tuhar explained that he understood and appreciated the opportunity to align with the Kingdom, as many of his residents were farmers and not soldiers. Tuhar even offered a strategic solution that Tutankhamun would implement immediately. They would build a tunnel along the west bank to the village that would serve as an underground route for the soldiers to attack the enemy from behind and possibly surround the enemy in battle. This strategy would improve their probability of victory against their enemies particularly if they designed several underground tunnels to other area villages.

As the evening progressed, governor Tuhar's wife called Tutankhamun, David, her husband, and the caravan into their great hall for a grand dinner. The night was filled with great food, great laughter, and dancing. At dinner, Tutankhamun was placed at the head of the table, out of respect, while Imani sat four seats away from him. David sat next to Tutankhamun watching him stare at her until she made eye contact and he would then look at David.

By the end of the evening, Tuhar brought his daughter to Tutankhamun. Tuhar explained that it was customary for the host family to offer a gift to the King. Imani, who was standing beside her family spoke softly and firmly as she presented the King a gift. Imani explained that the gift was made for their family more the two generations before by the chief architect of the village. He had found a reservoir of gold on his travels through the caves and with the gold carved out the blessings he wanted to bestow on the family and the village. All sides of the box including the top and bottom represented a season of blessing. One side represented the blessings for the crops with a picture of wheat representing a bountiful harvest. One side represented the blessing of the family with the bird peering over the gathering of our families. One side represented the blessing of peace with a rainbow on the horizon with the animals living in peace. One side represented love with a mother and father holding a child, and the top of the box representing RA and God.

As Imani stepped forward to hand Tutankhamun the box his hand touched her hand. Imani looked up from kneeling into Tutankhamun's eyes and David, standing beside them knew this would be the true love in Tutankhamun's life.

Tutankhamun's caravan left the following day, but not before he expressed to Tuhar that he would personally oversee the construction of the tunnel and would be making a weekly trip to the village until the tunnels were completed. Tuhar was pleased and asked that Tutankhamun and his caravan stay with him and his family during each visit. Tutankhamun agreed to the accommodations and asked that he be allowed to pay Tuhar and his family for their hospitality.

Upon Tutankhamun's return to the Kingdom, he was greeted by AY after he had placed the gold box by his bedside with all other gifts he had received on his Ambassador trip. AY informed him that after this trip he would no longer be allowed to journey to the villages and would rather that David continued in Tutankhamun's place. Tutankhamun was furious, as termination of his trips to the villages would prevent him from seeing or spending time with Imani. For the first time since Tutankhamun became King, he refused to take orders from AY. Now twelve years of age, Tutankhamun no longer needed AY's permission to assume his rightful position as King. He no longer had to take orders from AY.

Tutankhamun told AY that he was now the

King of Egypt and he would now take responsibility for necessary kingdom decisions. The villages were willing to help fortify the Kingdom and that he would oversee the fortification process. AY stood in disbelief as he watched the child he had raise since the death of his parents now give orders to him. AY apologized for overstepping his boundaries and stated that he was only looking out for the best interest of the Kingdom by offering a chance for Tutankhamun and Ankhesenamun to conceive an heir for the kingdom. Tutankhamun thanked his mentor for his concern and assured AY that he was doing what was best for the kingdom by continuing his work with the villages to fortify the city. The two agreed, and over the next twelve months, Tutankhamun visited the home of Governor Tuhar every week.

With each passing week, the friendship and the love between Imani and Tutankhamun grew stronger. While the diggers were working on the tunnels, Imani would take Tutankhamun on walks around the village and into the fields. They laid together in the wheat crops where no one could see them and they could talk about their feelings for each other. Imani, who was also twelve told Tutankhamun that the first night they met, when he touched her hand, she knew she loved him.

CHAPTER FIVE

I AM THE MORNING STAR

At the moment when the words rolled off of Imani's tongue, the weight of the world seemed to lift off of King Tutankhamun's shoulders. It did not matter that he was the most powerful man in the Egyptian universe. It did not matter what everyone, including his mentor and advisor AY expected of him, or his sister/wife Ankhesenamun, nor his father who now lived among the great kings of the great kings in the other world. The only being that mattered to Tutankhamun was this beautiful girl named Imani, whom he could see the light of the Gods in her eyes. Imani, the girl who would be his future, the future of the Kingdom of Egypt.

Tutankhamun kissed Imani on her forehead, took her hand and led her off to her home. He explained to her that he would need to return to the kingdom at once to tend to the business of his kingdom. As Tutankhamun and Imani returned to Imani's home he requested time to speak with Tuhar alone. Tuhar honored the king's request and led him to a quiet room in the rear of his home. Imani, returned to her room feeling light and happy, as she normally felt after spending an afternoon with her king, her love Tutankhamun. From her room, she heard Tutankhamun making his way to leave their home, and she ran to the doorway to catch a glimpse of Tutankhamun leaving. Her anxiousness increased waiting for the next time she would see Tutankhamun again.

Tutankhamun returned to the Kingdom with David at his side. They did not speak about the Kings early return to the Kingdom except for the request from Tutankhamun for David to stay by his side while he talked with AY. As Tutankhamun approached the gates, his resolve grew stronger; he knew it was time to take the reins of his rule. As his chariot passed the obelisks, David felt the shift in the atmosphere between he and Tutankhamun, as he watched his friend tighten his grip on the reigns of the chariot. He glanced up at Tutankhamun and watched his full lips tighten into a thin line on his face. His friend would change the dynamic of the Kingdom on this day.

As was tradition; AY greeted Tutankhamun in the great hall which was just inside the entrance. AY, typically stone-faced and ready to update the King on the events that happened when he was away, visibly shifted to a stance of discomfort watching Tutankhamun approach. AY could not wait until Tutankhamun reached him he stated in a slightly elevated voice, "Welcome home my King how was your journey to the villages?"

Tutankhamun ignored AY's greeting and responded in earnest, "I need Ankhesenamun removed from the Queens chambers, but accommodated as a member of the Royal Court. I have decided to take a wife, that I will elevate as my Queen."

AY tried not to look stunned by Tutankhamun's revelation but failed when he responded. "My King, you cannot remove Ankhesenamun as Queen, it is her rightful place as decided by your Father," AY responded then added. "Quite frankly, Tutankhamun you have no authority to remove a member of the Royal Court, you are in position as a family lineage of Royal blood, and unless the Queen meets with her untimely passing, you cannot remarry."

David watched his friend transform from indignation to fiery anger. Tutankhamun must have seen black in his anger because without warning Tutankhamun lunged at his mentor. Grabbing him by his arm and pulling him within an inch of his face. In a low voice, which Tutankhamun had never displayed in the past he leaned into AY, nearly resting his forehead on AY and said, "I am the morning star, I am he that will rest with the Gods in the hereafter, I am the rightful heir to the throne, I am endowed with all authority afforded by the Gods, I have all the authority necessary to change this kingdom and the world. You have overstepped your boundaries, but out of respect for you as my advisor and guide in this world, Nefertiti, and my Father, I will not order you killed for your disrespect of this kingdom. But make no mistake, this is my kingdom, and I will take a wife who will be Queen of Egypt."

Tutankhamun returned upright, release AY's arm, glared into his eyes and retired to his room. AY stood in the same spot looking stunned and embarrassed for a while Tutankhamun made his position as King very clear to AY, several priests and servants entered the great hall and observed the exchange between the mentor and his mentee who just took his rightful position as King.

David followed an obviously flustered King Tutankhamun to his room. David stood at the door in silence giving his friend, not his King or leader, time to calm down from his tirade. David watched his friend calm down, sit on his bed and then start to cry. David had never seen Tutankhamun cry, even when he was scared of being attacked in the Ethiopian war, or when he attended a funeral for a family member who died, or when he would get hit hard from combat training or fall off of his Chariot. For the first time in their relationship, he saw the vulnerable child who finally found something and someone to live for. David approached his friend Tutankhamun's' bedside, sat down slowly beside him to show that he was there to support him. Tutankhamun leaned on his friends' shoulder, which was incredibly unusual for the King, and allowed Tutankhamun to sob.

David and Tutankhamun sat in silence for what seemed like an eternity, with the occasional interruption from Tutankhamun staff who would be dismissed by David's waving his hand each time they attempted to enter the room. David would not allow his friend to become a spectacle for the kingdom. This was Tutankhamun's time to grieve the ending of a relationship with his second father and the beginning of a new life with the love of his life Imani.

CHAPTER SIX

TWO SIDES OF THE SAME COIN

David sat with his friend for what seemed like hours, ensuring Tutankhamun was resting. When Tutankhamun drifted off to sleep, David motioned to his staff to come into the room to service him. David rose from the bed exhausted and ready to retire to his chambers. As David exited Tutankhamun's room, he noticed movement to the left of him down the hall. As David lifted his head, heavy from feeling sleepy, he saw AY and his caravan moving with intention toward the front door of the Kingdom. David felt his body urge him to return to his quarters for much-needed rest, while also feeling his mind and the churning in his belly tell him that AY's intentions were going to put the kingdom in danger.

David turned to his left and rushed down the hall to see where AY and his caravan were going. By the time David made it down the corridor, he saw AY and caravan boarding horses and chariots then moving with haste toward the front gates. David made it to the front doors of the kingdom, just as AY and caravan were making a sand cloud from the hoofs of the horses as they ran swiftly past the Obelisks toward the front gates. The churning in David's stomach grew stronger and more irritating. He stopped and thought about going back and telling Tutankhamun about AY's movement. He also thought, perhaps he should tell the army commanders to wake from their beds and follow AY. The only problem with that idea was that he had nothing but the churning in his stomach, telling him something was wrong. Instead, David decided to tell the attendant, who assisted AY and his caravan, to get him a horse as swiftly as possible. He would follow AY himself and see if he could find proof that AY was about to put the kingdom in danger.

David followed the caravan to

Tutankhamun's recently completed tunnels. AY and the caravan picked the tunnel which led to Khuhua. David thought, perhaps he was overreacting, and AY was simply testing the tunnels for safety and fortification. Even as David thought positive about AY's motives, he also had the thought that perhaps he intended to hurt Imani. The thought that AY might hurt Imani made David feel sicker. He must get to Khuhua; he must make sure that nothing happens to her because Tutankhamun would be crushed. After all, he was willing to put his entire kingdom on the line for this woman and this love.

David reached the end of the tunnel and into Khuhua well after AY, and his caravan left the tunnel entrance. When David arrived at the entrance to the tunnel in Khuhua, it was early morning, and the sun had just peaked over the horizon lighting up the sky. David knew this was the time merchants and members of the governing party were leaving their homes. Tuhar and his wife would soon be traveling to the central governing building, but Imani and her brother would be at home sleeping. David did not see AY and the Caravan, but he made his way to the home of Tuhar with haste.

David arrived at the rear of the home of Tuhar. He saw a member of the caravan in the bushes to the left of the front gate of the home of Tuhar. As David scanned the area, he saw other members of the caravan crouched down in the surrounding shrubbery in attack mode. David came closer to the front of the home of Tuhar and saw AY approaching the front door. David fearing for the worse decided he needed to stop AY, but how? David was a Captain in the Egyptian Army, but this position gave David no authority to interfere with the affairs of government. It would be considered high treason if any citizen even spoke to a member of the Kings court without permission. David had only moments before AY would come face to face with Imani and potentially kill her.

Still unseen from the rear of Tuhar's home, David thought this would be the end of his life, but he knew he had to intervene. David had only seconds before he would be noticed by AY or a member of his caravan, but what options did he have? David could stand by and watch the mother of the next generation of the kingdom die along with the heart of his friend and his King or risk his life for the sake of the future of the kingdom. David new the weight of the world rested on the next action he would take. With his heart beating fast and his mind running faster he decided to gain the attention of Imani and her brother along with everyone else in the community.

Probably due to the rustling sounds in the back of Tuhar's home, AY paused at the front door. As David did not hear a knock on the door, he assumed he had only seconds before AY dispatched a member of the caravan to investigate the rustling noise. David had started a fire in the rear of the home and began running behind all of the homes that ran adjacent to Tuhar's home. In the split seconds David had to think, he looked to the roof line of Tuhar's home and saw the air vents that provided cool air during the hot seasons in Egypt and kept heat in during the cold seasons. Smoke from the fire would immediately fill the homes through the vent circulation causing all of the citizens to awake and leave their homes. Just as David suspected, he saw a member of the caravan come to the back of Tuhar's home to inspect, but David was already three homes away. The dried leaves that caused the rustling sounds were perfect for a quick diversion with a fast-blooming fire. Due to the angle of the homes and the rising fire and smoke, the member of the caravan did not see David spreading the fire.

In no less than two minutes the local community was filled with citizens coming out of their homes with a dazed look in their eyes. Several of the men, who were not merchants or members of government and therefore had not left their homes until the fire, signaled to each other to alert the governing councils for guidance and containment. Other men took water to the fire attempting to put it out and make sure it did not spread. David mingled with the crowd to remain undetected and move towards the home of Tuhar. From about 200 yards he saw AY stand firm at the home of Tuhar waiting for Imani to open the door. David watched the door from afar waiting as well for Imani to open the door. Other community members were coming to join the mob of people that were trying to find out about the fire, yet still no Imani.

David's tummy began to churn again thinking perhaps he went too far with the fire, and perhaps Tuhar's vent did not work like everyone else's, and he was now responsible for killing Imani and her brother. Perhaps they were trapped in the house and could not see clearly to the front door. With each passing second, David thought the worse, and looked up at AY standing at the front door growing increasingly more uncomfortable as time went on without a greeting at the door. Finally, out of the corner of David's eyes, he saw a glimmer of light in the high grass behind Tuhar's home. The glimmer of light looked like a reflection of daylight on some shiny object. Dawn had just crested and each moment reflected a little more daylight allowing him to see, even through the haze of smoke, two bodies crouching in the tall grass. David squinted his eyes and made out the bracelets Imani wore somedays they had visited over the past year.

David turned around to make his way through the ever-growing crowd of men, women, and children who were working frantically to put out the fire David had set. David ran back about 5 houses and then turned left to cut between the houses and enter the tall grass that aligned all of the houses adjacent to Tuhar's home. David crouched through the tall grass making his way in the direction of Imani. It took about three seconds for David to find her, she had stopped and got low in the grass. When David reached Imani, she explained in a whisper voice that a member of the Caravan had spotted movement in the grass and started to explore the grass, if she and her brother were to go deeper into the grass and remain low and still, they would likely go undetected. Imani was relieved to see David, but as she looked at David's face, she knew she must have been in grave danger.

David led Imani back on the path he had taken to find her in the grass, in hopes that if they were far enough away from Imani's home, they could easily blend into the community and out of danger. Just as pregnant Imani emerged from the grassy area behind her home, she came face to face with AY and his caravan. David emerged behind Imani and then stood beside her and her brother. AY eyed each of them suspiciously in silence for a moment. With the caravan members at AY's side, the first to speak was Imani.

"What a pleasant surprise to see you here near our home and on such a strange morning in our community," Imani said, trying not to sound suspicious.

AY responded saying, "Yes, this is peculiar to have a fire on the morning of my visit to your home, but the purpose of my visit is more pressing than the fires that appear to have been intentionally started. Can we retire to your courtyard to speak?"

Imani, apparently considering her response carefully, asked if she could fetch her father before discussing matters of the state outside of his presence. AY looked at Imani's brother

Steven and ordered him to fetch his father. Steven, understanding the respect required for AY's position, did not hesitate to agree to fetch his father and began walking in the direction of his father's location in the central government. Young Steven, Imani's brother walked 20 steps and came face to face with his father and mother. They had already been notified of the fires and was making their way back to their home to investigate.

AY had already led Imani, David, & his Caravan to Tuhar's courtyard to speak and failed to see that young Steven had already found his parents. AY wasted no time helping Imani know the purpose of his visit. He asked her directly about her relationship with the King and whether or not the child she was carrying was the King's child. David saw Imani's eyes that appeared to be filled with fear and tears. David felt helpless to both himself and Imani knowing that if he spoke for Imani to AY, he could be subject to death.

Imani sat in silence, contemplating her answer to AY, for the wrong answer would have terrible consequences for her, her love the king, her unborn child, and her family. She loved Tutankhamun more than breathing, but she did not want risk everyone's life because of the truth. Imani began to speak, "I do love Tutankhamun, and I understand he is the King of Egypt..." Her voice trailed off as she saw her father turn and walk into the courtyard.

Tuhar looked at his daughter, who appeared frightful and ready to cry and asked her in the calmest, fatherly voice to take her brother and retire into their home. Tuhar turned to AY, who appeared to want to rebuke Tuhar for defying him as he asked for information from his daughter, and told him to remove himself and his caravan from his courtyard. Tuhar explained further that he had watched the exchange between AY and Imani and felt his actions were disrespectful to his home. Tuhar also expressed that he would speak to the King about this disrespectful action and their future relationship with the Kingdom. Tuhar asked that David remain in his presence to assist in resolving the fire outbreak behind his home.

It took Tuhar several moments to speak to David, as he appeared to contemplate his words. Finally, Tuhar asked David, "was AY here to kill my daughter?"

David did not hesitate to answer Tuhar with, "Yes, he was." David continued to explain why, "When Tutankhamun returned to the Kingdom last evening he told AY that he would take Imani as his wife and move her into the Kingdom. After sharing this information with AY, AY got very angry, and Tutankhamun yelled at his lifelong mentor and father figure."

Tuhar's wife had retired to the rear of the home to put out the fire along with her servants, so she did not hear the explanation of AY's visit. Tuhar slowly sat down on the seat in his courtyard and remained silent as David sat down and they pondered for a long time. Finally, Tuhar responded, "It is settled, for the sake of the kingdom and the safety of our family we cannot keep this child. Imani, cannot move into the kingdom, and Tutankhamun must terminate his relationship with Imani. Their relationship will never be honored, and their child will never be recognized as the heir to the throne."

David continued to sit in silence knowing that Tuhar was right about the kingdom, but also that Tutankhamun would be displeased. How would David be able to explain what happened this morning to Tutankhamun, how would AY accept David back into his position as a Captain, and would Imani give up her child for the safety of her King, her family, and herself?

CHAPTER SEVEN

THE JOURNEY BACK

After speaking with Tuhar, David resigned to go and request the presence of Tutankhamun at Tuhar's home. Tuhar promised to reserve his conversation with Imani about the baby until King Tutankhamun returned with David.

The journey back to Egypt was a long one for David. As his horse carried him through the tunnels, out of the tunnels, and into the gates of the kingdom David stayed in deep thought. His thought briefly focused on how his life would be in danger if he were to speak against AY to the King, but his greater thoughts were on his friend and his king. David felt Tutankhamun deserved a life with Imani and their child. He thought that this was the opportunity to sit on the throne of his kingdom alongside his friend and his love. This was his opportunity to build his kingdom beyond his father Akhenaten, because he would be made whole with his love and his heir. David thought it was unfair for Tutankhamun, but he also considered the Egyptian traditions. The turmoil in his head weighed more heavily on him because he was physically exhausted from a lack of sleep that was now taking its toll on him. As he approached the kingdom doors, David felt the gravity of tears in his eyes for the pain he knew was coming when he told his friend the news.

David approached the doors of the kingdom and saw the rush of activity happening just beyond the doorway. When David reached the attendant that would assist with his horse, it was about noon and the day was very hot and bright from the sun that seemed to be shining straight onto his head. He dismounted his horse and wanted to slip in the right of the kingdom unnoticed so that he could slip up to his room.

As David crossed the threshold to the kingdom, he heard a voice call out "There He is, seize him."

David whirled around to see what was taking place, and as he turned, he was met by five army guards and the commander of the Army. David, looking astonished was speechless as he tried to grasp the nature of his fellow soldier's attack. The soldiers who grabbed David were all much older than him, and in his befuddled state, he recognized several of the soldiers as his trainers and mentors in the Army. He looked up to his right side to look the soldier who held his arm in the eyes; there was something peculiar about the look in his eyes. Finally, reason returned to David, and he thought this is AY's doing and uttered the words, as the soldiers were dragging him across the grand hall, "What have I done?" David's question brought the commander and the soldiers holding David to a halt.

The commander looked at David with a stern look touched by anger, which David had only seen in his commander during the war with Ethiopia. "You have committed treason and shall be committed to death," the Commander exclaimed.

All of David's fears came to life in an instant, he was going to die and had not told his friend the truth about his love, he was going to die at the hands of AY, and every life he was committed to saving from Imani, to Tuhar, to Tutankhamun would now perish. His death would have no meaning because he would die with a secret that would be the crossroads for the kingdom and his friend and king. Feeling as though he would collapse from utter exhaustion, David made himself ask the Commander, "Why?"

David's question must have reverberated through the soldiers, the Commander, and the kingdom because just as he uttered the words, there was what sounded like a mob of people coming down the hallway toward the grand hall. With the soldiers and commanders stopping to speak with David, he was able to feebly stand on his feet and was forced to look in the direction of the commotion heading his way.

Shortly after David stood to his feet, he saw the shiny breastplate of Tutankhamun turning left into the great hall. Tutankhamun was in a robust argument with AY, David discovered shortly after Tutankhamun turned the corner. The animated discussed between Tutankhamun and AY seemed focused on some information that AY shared and Tutankhamun expressing his great disbelief in the words spoken by his advisor and mentor.

Tutankhamun repeated several times; I will need to hear this for myself, your intentions seem misdirected. Tutankhamun had the look of a child who wanted to escape a teacher who told him he should believe simply because they said so. Whatever information Tutankhamun received from AY was apparently far too extraordinary to believe, and with the previous night's discussion, he was losing faith in the words of his advisor and mentor. AY looked as though he was trying to maintain his steely resolve as a trusted advisor and leader in the kingdom while also attempting to distract his mentee from the truth.

As Tutankhamun and AY turned the corner, they both appeared shocked at the site of

David being seized by members of the army and the head Military Commander. AY's look of shock came from believing David would have already been taken away and out of site from Tutankhamun. King Tutankhamun's look of shock appeared on his face out of shear bewilderment. Why was his friend being carried away like an enemy of Egypt?

King Tutankhamun steadied himself and glared at his advisor; he asked in a controlled anger laced voice, "What is happening here?" King Tutankhamun turned and faced AY while slowly asking the question. Tutankhamun's anger seeping through his skin did not visibly affect AY, but you could tell he was affected when he began to speak.

"King Tutankhamun, I requested this man be seized and put to death for treason against the kingdom." AY commanded, then continued, "This man set fire to the community of Khuhua threatening the lives of all members of the community and destroying our relationships you worked so hard to create, King Tutankhamun."

AY said King Tutankhamun's name, as if it tasted like vinegar coming out of his mouth.

Tutankhamun recognized the difficulty AY had saying his name and without hesitation, he ordered that David be released immediately. "This man will be brought up before the governing council of Khuhua and they will decide his fate," King Tutankhamun stated staring directly into AY eyes. King Tutankhamun finally recognized the power struggle that would now exist between he and AY; he understood that for the past three years AY ruled Egypt because Tutankhamun was too young. The only way this kingdom was going to work, was for Tutankhamun to force his way in as ruler of Egypt. The main advantage King Tutankhamun had was the message his father, King Akhenaten, gave him before he died, "a man's ruin lies on his tongue."

As Tutankhamun made his case as the King of Egypt in the presence of AY, the Commander of the Army, soldiers who had seized David, and David who watched his friend/

King transform from a child to the Great King of Egypt, several other priests, attendants, and servants made their way to the great hall. No one wanted to move once they arrived in the presence of the King, they did not want to call attention to themselves as the tension in the room between King Tutankhamun, and AY made the great hall suffocating.

King Tutankhamun was the first to move away from the great hall. But not without first commanding the Military commander and David to follow him to his wing of the kingdom. As they moved toward the hallway leading toward Tutankhamun's chambers, David noticed the noise of individuals moving and walking began to elevate in the great hall behind them. David peaked at his friend and King out of the corner of his left eye and saw the tension on his face, not of anger but great contemplation. David assumed it was because King Tutankhamun was strategizing his next move.

King Tutankhamun, David, and the military commander arrived in the Library of the first annex located in the east quadrant of the central building. In the library David watched his friend/king pace slowly for a moment and then provide detailed instructions to the military commander about taking David to Khuhua to present him to the governing body. Tutankhamun told the commander to collect 20 of his best soldiers to journey with the King's caravan to the City of Khuhua. These soldiers would be responsible for surrounding the King, David, and the king's servants during the journey. The King informed the commander that he was not to allow any person other than who the King expressly stated to be near the traveling caravan. The King went on, stating that when they arrived in Khuhua soldiers are to surround the family of Tuhar to ensure their safety. A small group of soldiers are to stay with The King, David, and Tuhar as we traveled to the governing council's office. As King Tutankhamun concluded speaking with the military commander he closed by telling him each time they meet with the governing council of Khuhua the soldiers are to dismiss themselves from the discussions.

King Tutankhamun dismissed the military commander telling him to speak of their conversation with no other individual including AY. The military commander nodded in agreement and retired from the Kings' presence to prepare the caravan for military protection. Tutankhamun returned his gaze to David and told him to prepare to leave within the hour for Khuhua. Now alone, Tutankhamun explained to David that he was very aware of his innocence and intent to save Imani, but he needed David to tell him what made him follow AY that morning.

Exhausted David explained how the past hours have been exhausting and exhilarating at the same time. David told Tutankhamun that as he left his room the previous night he saw a group of soldiers making their way to the front of the great hall in a manner with which he was trained. When the soldiers are called to engage in war or battle activity, their formations are close and staggered with at least two rows of soldiers. When David looked at the caravan of soldiers following AY he noticed their formation and the body armor, both of which indicated they would be engaging in some hand to hand combat. David expressed concern because of the heated discussion between Tutankhamun and AY. With all these details in mind, David decided to follow AY and the caravan.

David continued to tell Tutankhamun that the closer he got to Khuhua the greater his concern for Imani and her family. Being a soldier in the army meant that David could have joined the caravan that night, David thought, but he knew he needed to be separate from the Army to find a way to protect Imani if he needed to. He could not protect them if he were accounted for as a member of the caravan. David told Tutankhamun, he wanted to come back and tell him what was going on, but there was no time. King Tutankhamun understood the urgency by nodding for David to continue with his story, even though he spoke no words while David spoke.

David continued to tell Tutankhamun about how he had to act quickly when he saw AY at the door, and the soldiers crouched in the bushes ready to attack. As David grew closer to telling King Tutankhamun about the circumstances surrounding his setting the fire Tutankhamun's face changed from impassive to fear to shear anger. As David closed the story with the interaction between AY and Imani and then between AY and Tuhar, King Tutankhamun looked as though he would jump out of his skin. The king was ready to protect his legacy!

David had no time to retire to his chambers. Instead, Tutankhamun ordered one of his servants to fetch personal items for David and himself and load them into the caravan. After the conversation with David, King Tutankhamun retired to his chambers changed into his formal attire and then made his way to the front gate of the great hall. King Tutankhamun approaching the front gate noticed AY in an annex to the right of the great hall just behind a half-closed door. King Tutankhamun could not see the person AY was speaking with but recognized the normally contained AY speaking in an animated motion as if to showcase his anger. King Tutankhamun noticed he never looked up to see the King passing by. He continued to the caravan chariot and boarded alongside his friend.

As they journeyed to Khuhua through the tunnels King Tutankhamun was pleased with the work done by the military commander, as he had done exactly as instructed. The soldiers flanked him on each side and commanded the entire caravan as if they would readily attack anyone that remotely appeared to want to approach or attack this group.

The caravan arrived in Khuhua just before dusk and saw a commotion occurring at the home of Tuhar. There were a few chariots outside of Tuhar's home along with several servant groups. As they approached the military commander slowed their caravan, jumped off the chariot with two other soldiers and advanced to the home of Tuhar. King Tutankhamun watched from his chariot neatly tucked behind the bushes that had grown over the entrance of the tunnel. The military commander approached the front gate of governor Tuhar's home and was stopped by a servant watching the gate. The commander announced that he was from King Tutankhamun's court and the servant immediately stepped back as if they felt they would be beheaded for stopping a member of the king's court. The commander turned away from the servant, and he and the two soldiers advanced to the front door. Just as they arrived two members of the government opened an exited the front door only pausing for a moment when they stood face to face with the Kings soldiers. As they stood still at the door Tuhar, who was sitting at the back of the room looked up and recognized the commander from AY's caravan.

Tuhar was ready this time to make it very clear to AY he was NOT welcome at his home or on his property. Tuhar stood and motioned with his left hand to others in the room to follow him to the front door. As they made haste across the floor six men, 2 of whom were local soldiers met the military commander at the door. Ready to make it known that his presence will not be tolerated by the community of Khuhua, Tuhar glanced up and saw King Tutankhamun entering the gates with David. Tuhar looked at the commander, who remained indifferent standing at his door and motioned for everyone he had brought to the door to back up.

Tutankhamun approached the door with his anger elevated, not at Tuhar, but at the realization that because he was the King of Egypt, he would need to give up the most precious things in his life to keep them and the family safe. Tuhar looked past King Tutankhamun to see David who looked like he had been involved in a personal battle. Tuhar gave David a slight smile to let him know he was truly thankful for whatever he endured bringing Tutankhamun to his home. Tuhar greeted Tutankhamun after the military commander stepped to the side yet still in protection mode.

Tutankhamun entered the home of Tuhar amongst a throng of people he did not recognize. Although these people resembled members of the noble class, based on their clothes and manner, he felt strangely simultaneously welcome and out of place. Tuhar, feeling the uneasiness of his friend began introducing both King Tutankhamun and

David to fellow members of the governing council of Khuhua. Tuhar explained that everyone had gathered to discuss the newly embattled relationship between Khuhua and AY the Kings Vizier. Tuhar went on to explain that everyone in the room was aware of the fire and its purpose, so there was no need to proceed with the prosecution of David as an enemy of Khuhua. Instead, the governing council considers the bravery of David to be an act of peace between our communities.

David felt a sigh of relief but wondered how Tutankhamun would smooth things back at the Kingdom. How, would the King resolve the issues between David and AY and ensure AY would not try to kill David in the future? David was distracted from his thoughts when King Tutankhamun asked for a private audience with Imani.

Tuhar explained that Imani was not present in the room to reduce the speculation about the child. No one other than himself, his wife, King Tutankhamun, and David knew the reality about the child. The community understands that there was an issue between AY an Tuhar relating to decisions made by the family to embrace the King and all of the king's gifts, but they were not aware of the true story about the child.

CHAPTER EIGHT

DO I KNOW YOU?

King Tutankhamun stepped into Imani's room; it felt like he had not seen her in months when their time apart was only days. Imani had her back to 13-year-old King Tutankhamun and as she turned around, he felt as happy as a child. He felt like his life went back too normal when he saw her face and her protruding belly which held an entire nation within it. Imani did not speak but rather approached King Tutankhamun with the grace of a queen and a gentleness of a best friend. Alone with Imani was the only place King Tutankhamun wanted to be. Even though he knew the weight of the world, rested on his shoulders at this moment he did not care. The love of his life made it to his arms, and he felt completely at home.

Imani rested her head on his chest and appeared to be counting his heartbeats with the intensity of a scientist. She grew closer to King Tutankhamun until her entire body, including the side of her belly, rested on him. She too understood the weight of the moment, that she held a kingdom inside her, but she just wanted to savor this moment for as long as possible.

David broke the silence and the silent sound of the moment by entering the room with Tuhar and Anai, Tuhar's wife. David stood in the corner of the room while Imani, Tuhar, Anai, and Tutankhamun sat in the available chairs. The tension in the room was thick as they all understood the breadth of the moment, they would need to decide the fate of the child Imani was carrying. This decision would affect everyone in the room as this would be the individuals who would be trusted with the secret of the kingdom for possibly a lifetime.

Tuhar glanced around the room to see both Imani and Anai crying, while Tutankhamun looked choked up with emotion. David refused to make eye contact with the governor as he tried to contain his own emotion. Tuhar in a low whispering voice fought through the emotion in his throat to say, "We have to decide, tonight. We cannot risk the life of this child nor can we continue to put the lives of our family in danger."

When Tuhar said this, King Tutankhamun's eye shot up and made contact with Tuhar. Tutankhamun knew he was right; he grabbed Imani's hand as she sat to the left of him and said, "I would not want to live if anything happened to you we have to do what is best. I thought the best thing would be to bring you to the kingdom and take you as my queen but I now know that would not be safer it would put you and this life," he touched Imani's belly, "in more danger than ever." As Tutankhamun spoke, Imani cried harder knowing that she would have to let this beautiful life inside her go.

Immediately after Tutankhamun spoke, Anai startled everyone with a scream. Everyone in the room seemed to move in unison to see what was wrong with Anai. She stood up, faced Tuhar and said Salihah and Lateef. Everyone else in the room looked puzzled and remained quiet as Anai explained. Lateef is the chief council of water for our community, and his wife Salihah is pregnant with their second child. Salihah and Imani are friends and have spent most days together. If we ask Lateef and Salihah to take the baby, Imani could help with the baby and keep a relationship as the child grows. Both Salihah and Imani share the same midwife who would keep the births a secret and safe. I know everyone in this room wants to see the child grow up. Our son Steven and Salihah's son Firesky are friends and spend many nights together and since their babies would be the same age as this child they could raise them as twins and no one would ever know. The room stayed quiet as everyone stayed quiet and in shock.

Imani spoke first through the tears, "I think that is a great idea. I don't want to lose our child Tutankhamun," Imani looked intently at King Tutankhamun. Imani continued," by giving our child to Salihah and Lateef we stay connected without anyone knowing. If I say I lost the baby after the child is born, no one will be aware."

Tutankhamun remained still as if he was stunned by the idea and kept his head low while also holding Imani's hand. His body sunk as if defeated by the idea. This was a no-win situation, and Tutankhamun knew it. He finally raised his head and sullenly said, I agree let us make this request of the family. Tutankhamun then rose and adjourned to the next room which was the library. Although there was a gathering at the home of Governor Tuhar, the library was empty. Tutankhamun was soon joined by Imani alone. She stood at the door of the library, tears streaming down her cheek, watching her love process the news of a situation he could not control. Her sweet words to him seemed to be all he needed to return to the present, "We are in control of making our child safe, you are a great king because you know the blessing of sacrifice for the good of others, the child will always be our love." Tutankhamun turned and embraced Imani as if he was soaking her into his skin.

After their embrace, they heard the door

open, and a woman of middle age entered. Her face seemed familiar to Tutankhamun although his brain could not seem to register from where. She resembled a servant but with silk linings that reflected she might have worked for royalty. Imani turned and extended her hand to who she introduced as Nekteri her midwife. Nekteri took Imani's hand and came closer to Imani and Tutankhamun. Tutankhamun could not help but acknowledge how familiar Nekteri looked to him and finally asked the question, "Do I know you?"

Nekteri nodded at the king, and with Imani watching with a shocked look, she said, "I was your midwife and teacher at the kingdom, sire." Nekteri never looked Tutankhamun in the eyes, as she felt it disrespectful to lay eyes on the King. Tutankhamun recognized his teacher as she finished her explanation. A wave of relief fell upon Tutankhamun as his previous fear of the midwife being the one to tell AY about the child was now dashed. Every worker at the kingdom was sworn to a lifetime of secrecy or suffer immediate death.

Imani too was relieved to know that the midwife had a vested interest in their secret and would be more likely to keep the secret for a lifetime. Imani asked Nekteri to take a seat and proceeded to explain the current situation with the pregnancy and their desire to give the unborn child to Salihah and Lateef. She went onto explain this must be treated with the utmost secrecy from everyone except those in the house of Tuhar, King Tutankhamun alone and David along with Salihah and Lateef. The midwife understood as she was responsible for similar secrets in the house of Akhenaten, Tutankhamun's father. As Imani completed speaking with Nekteri, as if on cue, Tuhar and Anai entered the room with Salihah, Lateef and David.

When Imani finished explaining the situation and the request to Salihah and Lateef they sat in silence looking back and forth to each with a look of shear disbelief. After a few moments, Salihah looked at Imani and asked;

"Are you sure? You Love this baby."

Imani nodded her head yes, and then responded; "As long as you will allow us to watch this child grow!"

Salihah, whether because of her emotional state or shear shock, began to cry. The crying became so uncontrollable that she put her head in her hands and starting weeping. The realization that Imani and Tutankhamun were willing to entrust her and Lateef with the life of their unborn child was overwhelming. Lateef leaned to his left and put his arm around his weeping wife. He knew there was nothing else to say, Salihah's weeping answered the question, Yes, we would take the baby as our own and make sure that Imani and Tutankhamun were always in this child's life to watch it grow.

CHAPTER NINE

WHERE THE KINGS LIVE FOREVER

The next few months seemed to move like a symphony that everyone involved knew how to play. Imani would wake each morning, bathe and dress her ever-increasingly swollen body, leave her home and spend the day with Salihah. The two would talk at length about their hopes and wishes for their unborn children. The two would watch Firesky, Salihah's son and his friend Steven, Imani's brother finish their school lessons with their tutor. Around midday they would gather their friends the twin boys Aaron and Apollo who were a year younger than Firesky and one female child that did not attend school due to tradition, named Miriam and steal away to the edge of the Nile. No one knew what the friends did daily, but whatever it was they would return in fits of laughter as if they escaped capture from their daily mischief.

As the sun went down each day Imani feeling satisfied would return home with her brother Steven to meet their parents and begin the process of preparing for dinner. Dinners were filled with lighthearted discussions about the activities taking place in the city primarily focused on preparing for the next season of harvest. Tuhar, Imani's father, was responsible for ensuring a successful planting and harvesting season. This was the beginning of the harvesting season, following Akhet – the inundation or flooding season, and there was much work to be done. Children just older than Steven and Firesky were working with their families to plant wheat, corn, flax, melons, along with other fruits and vegetables. Tuhar shared the challenges he would face each day supporting the local farmers who needed more grain or more land or more help. Each of his days were filled with solving village farmer's issues. Imani would relish in the conversations held during dinner and also day dream of what Tutankhamun's days were filled with.

David would visit the home of Tuhar each week. He was unofficially sent by Tutankhamun to check on Imani, to see how she and his heir were progressing. Each week David would sit and talk with Imani alone to not only gather information to report back to Tutankhamun but also to gather the personal letters written from Imani to Tutankhamun. Officially, David would take time with Tuhar to discuss matters of government and ways that Egypt could provide aid to the city of Khuhua.

Each time David would return to King Tutankhamun, the King would leave the main grounds with him and journey to a Gazebo along the Nile river. The King would be followed by his servants and two fellow guards who were trusted by Tutankhamun. The caravan would walk approximately 1 meter behind David and Tutankhamun which allowed them to speak with the most privacy. David would read his report to Tutankhamun, who in turn would simply beam with pride in the knowledge that both his love and his heir were safe and happy.

After David would read his report to Tutankhamun, he would give Imani's letter to him. On only one occasion did Tutankhamun read the letter aloud to David, which read as follows:

My dearest love I dream each day of our life together. In my dreams, you are the sun, and you provide light for every part of my life. I feel our child growing inside and know that the plans we forged while lying in the wheat fields will come true even if we are not physically together. The day is coming soon that our child will arrive and I know you cannot be here to hold them I will blow a kiss to RA to deliver to your lips. Our families will forever be connected, and our amulet will remain as a symbol of our enduring commitment to each other. As sweet as the melon in the sun, so is the sweet smell of love on my tongue for you. If ever you cannot find me here, know that I am on the hill in the far east horizon where the kings live forever. With Love from your heart.

Tutankhamun read the letter three times and got lost in the melody of the words. He pulled the letter to his golden breastplate, which lay over his linen tunic, one last time and closed his eyes. His daytime dream of Imani was interrupted by the sounds of marching feet coming closer to him. King Tutankhamun quickly opened his eyes and saw on the horizon beyond the glare of the sun, a group of soldiers moving closer to him at the Gazebo. He had not ordered any military exercise today and wondered about the commotion.

As the soldiers moved closer he recognized the head of the soldier regime was the Army Commander, the same commander who had captured David in the great hall after AY attempted to kill Imani in Khuhua. David watched Tutankhamun become tense, even though no one else could see the change through Tutankhamun's linen tunic and long shendyt wrap which fell below his knees. The Commander stopped one-half meter from King Tutankhamun and reported that factions of soldiers were seen 20 kilometers from the kingdom to the south. The commander requested an audience alone with the King to brief him on the situation and request permission to approach the visiting soldiers to determine the soldier's intent and avoid any conflict. King Tutankhamun handed his letter to David and with David at his side stepped to the right of the Gazebo closest to the Nile about 1 meter from the group of soldiers and his attendants.

The Army commander informed King Tutankhamun and David that they saw the soldiers on the horizon to the north for the past 48 hours. We have been watching the soldiers who appear to be waiting for something or someone. They are approximately five kilometers from tunnels at Elreyah. We could take our soldiers through the tunnels and come out behind the visiting soldiers, and if they are hostile; we could take the advantage.

King Tutankhamun looked to be weighing his options and asked the most important question to the Army commander, "What if the line you see from a distance is only the front of the brigade, like pawns in Chess, and are awaiting your arrival to take over the Kingdom?" The Commander, with all of his battle strategy and military experience dating back to Akhenaten, looked as if he smelled something foul and looked in awe of King Tutankhamun's strategic mind all at the same time. He paused and considered his answer to the King with great patience, and responded to King Tutankhamun with more of a question than his usual affirmative answer. The commander said, "I believe we should take much caution in approaching the visiting soldiers, take three brigades of soldiers through the tunnels and approach the visiting soldiers with a single brigade in the event there are more visiting soldiers awaiting our first move. If there are more visiting soldiers waiting, our second and third brigade should be sufficient to hold down their forces and notify additional Egyptian brigades if necessary who will be waiting at the entrance of the tunnel on the kingdom side." King Tutankhamun looked intently at the Commander and simply nodded his white-crown covered head.

The Commander turned back to his faction

of soldiers and guided them past King Tutankhamun and his attendees in a hurried fashion. King Tutankhamun, looking disappointed, turned to David and instructed him to return to the kingdom and join the commander in his efforts to determine the intention of the visiting soldiers on the horizon. He then turned to his attendees and had them rush him back to his chambers. David caught King Tutankhamun saying to his attendees that he would be joining the commander and would need to be dressed in war gear. David, who was in mid-step moving towards the kingdom stopped abruptly, turned around, and addressed King Tutankhamun with the most sternness and respect he could muster.

"My King, the commander and I will take care of this for you; please return to your chambers until we can confirm the kingdom is out of danger," David told King Tutankhamun.

David paused, as if to contemplate his remaining response, and said "the future of your kingdom depends on this moment."

King Tutankhamun, understood what his friend meant, as David returned Imani's letter to him. His eyes began to water in a way that only he and David understood and then responded to David in a careful tone. "Please ensure I am kept up to date on the status of your meeting." David nodded, turned and hurried to meet the commander.

King Tutankhamun returned to the kingdom and walked to the western chambers where Ankhesenamun resided. Tutankhamun did not knock on her chamber doors. Instead, he crossed the threshold after her attendees opened the door and bowed their heads upon seeing the King approaching. Ankhesenamun who was in her dressing chamber heard the activity at the door and knew right away it was Tutankhamun. She entered her main room area with a white linen tunic with a hem that kissed the floor. Tutankhamun approached her with a loving smile and kissed her on her cheek then stepped back from her. Ankhesenamun responded to his silent address verbally, "To what do I owe this great honor that you would come to my chambers without an invitation?" King Tutankhamun and Ankhesenamun sat in wooden chairs covered with silk seat covers, and they discussed the soldiers who were posted on the eastern horizon 20 kilometers from the kingdom. Tutankhamun shared with Ankhesenamun that he would provide extra protection for her and her attendants and that they were to remain in the western wing of the kingdom until they were no longer in danger. The two sat and talked for a while about the events they were participating in and then King Tutankhamun retired to his chambers. King Tutankhamun knew he would have to protect his queen Ankhesenamun from danger, with this understanding of protecting the kingdom from an eminent danger he also knew it would seem like a lifetime before he could see Imani again. After that he clung to his letters from Imani in hopes that they would be his lifeline until they could see each other again.

CHAPTER TEN

MY KING, I BRING NEWS

The military, led by Commander Horemheb, journeyed through the tunnels at Elreyah. A small faction of the soldiers including Commander Horemheb and David slipped unseen out of the tunnels and took positions behind the high weeds of the receding Nile to see the visiting soldiers. As King Tutankhamun suspected there were lines of soldiers posted directly behind the soldiers who could be seen from the kingdom. As Commander Horemheb began to count the number of soldiers he stopped at 100 and recognized the symbols on their shields as Hittite. Commander Horemheb, being a student of modern warfare, determined that there were several legions of soldiers positioning themselves to attack the Kingdom of Egypt. Commander Horemheb, careful to remain unseen slipped back into the tunnels to consider his options for advancement to overtake the Hittite militia and protect the Kingdom. Commander Horemheb, David, and other leaders moved back into the tunnel about 1 meter to discuss their strategy. Commander Horemheb instructed David to lead a team of 20 soldiers back to the Kingdom to inform King Tutankhamun and ready no less than 200 soldiers with full artillery to join them in the tunnel.

Commander Horemheb grabbed David's forearm and engaged David's eyes and commanded, "You have to close all other tunnels for the safety of the communities."

David looked bewildered at Commander Horemheb for a second longer than normal, as his thoughts immediately strayed to Imani and King Tutankhamun's unborn heir. Did Commander Horemheb know about Imani and King Tutankhamun's heir? If the Commander knew why hadn't he killed Imani to preserve the legacy of Egypt. David gathered himself saluted the Commander and returned to the Kingdom with the 20 soldiers to carry out Horemheb's orders.

David arrived back at the kingdom just after midday and knew that Tutankhamun, AY, and the priest would be in meeting at this time. David journeyed to the east courtyard Temple. Here the priests and leaders would gather to make offerings to the Gods and under the blessing of the Gods discuss the needs of the Kingdom. David respectfully entered the grand room where more than 40 sat at the table with King Tutankhamun at the head.

David entered the room with only five of the soldiers he had led back from the tunnels flanked on either side of him, Tutankhamun and AY immediately switched their gaze from the table to David. David bowed and then approached the table. David stated, "My King, I bring news from Commander Horemheb." King Tutankhamun slightly bowed his white-crowned head granting David the opportunity to share his news with himself along with the leaders in the room.

David taking notice that all of the leaders were in white linen representing worship and a cleansing occurring, continued to speak. "My King, as you suspected the soldiers posted 20 kilometers to the east are only the beginning of the Army of the Hittites. The soldiers are perfectly aligned behind one another to the count of more than one hundred soldiers. Commander Horemheb decreed that we gather no less than 200 of our soldiers in full artillery to advance through the tunnels to fight and protect the Kingdom. Commander Horemheb also decreed that we close all of the tunnels except those at Elreyah for the safety of those in the cities, should the Hittites advance to ensure the tunnels stay undetected."

As David informed the group that they would need to close the tunnel he squinted his eyes at Tutankhamun in hopes that Tutankhamun would grasp the notion that he would not be able to visit Imani until the Kingdom and all surrounding communities were out of danger. David stood ready to debate the strategy decreed by Commander Horemheb, but all persons in the room sat quietly, no one inquired or added a word of advice. AY looked to be contemplating other options, as he was the only person in the room, David recognized, with any military or combat experience. As David bowed to the King he looked at Tutankhamun who had sadness in his eyes. David felt the pain for King Tutankhamun, but then saw him collect himself and nod his approval for Commander Horemheb's strategy.

Imani happened to be walking across the courtyard of her father's home when she heard the commotion at the gates to the tunnels. She walked through the courtyard gates and walked around the shrubbery to the right outside the gates and saw Egyptian soldiers closing and locking the tunnel gate. A pregnant Imani walked gingerly to the gates and asked the soldiers who were on the inside of the gates why were these gates being closed and locked? By the time she made it to the gates other members of the community noticed the commotion and were making their way to the gates to inquire as well, including Imani's brother Steven and Lateef, Salihah's husband. The Egyptian soldiers informed the small crowd that by decree of King Tutankhamun all tunnel gates were too be closed as a militia from the east attempted to invade.

Imani glared at Lateef like she was looking through him in deep thought. When she came to her senses, she knew something was wrong as Lateef was never at home at this time in the morning. Lateef, recognizing the confusion on her face stated, "I was coming to gather you, something is wrong with Salihah." Imani looked down at Steven and told him to tell their parents about the gates, and that she would be at the home of Salihah and Lateef. Imani followed Lateef around the corner while Steven took off running to the Governing offices to tell his parents about the tunnels.

Imani and Lateef arrived in the main room to see Salihah lay on a bench woven with hafra grass and topped with a cushion of thick linen stuffed with feathers. The Midwife, Nekteri, had already arrived and Firesky had been sent away with his tutor to engage in his lessons outside of the home. Salihah was crying and struggling through the pain she was experiencing. Imani walked over first to Nekteri who was feeling on Salihah's belly with a worried look on her face. Nekteri said no words, but even young Imani knew there was something terrible happening. Imani looked up at Lateef who was standing like a statute across the room with his hand to his mouth. She began to walk over to Lateef and was suddenly struck by a sharp pain, grabbed her belly with her right hand and bent over and grabbed the chair to her left.

Lateef came out of his statute like pose and reached out to Imani to help her into the chair she grabbed. Imani was able to position herself into the chair and took several deep breaths. In the midst of recovering herself through deep breaths, she told Lateef to go outside and wait. She asked him to collect the other midwives Nekteri had instructed both families to have them ready to assist if the children arrived at similar times. Lateef left the house and gathered the help of the other local midwives, three in total, who would help with the needs of the delivery. Shortly after Lateef left the house, the three women entered, and Lateef stayed waiting in their courtyard nervously.

Imani's pain subsided mildly, and she went to Salihah's side, applying cold compresses to her head as Nekteri continued to attend to her pain. Nekteri had Salihah moved from the bench to the delivery pad in the annex to their home as it was time for the baby to arrive. Imani joined Salihah and Nekteri while the other women waited outside the door. Imani's pain began to increase, but she dismissed it staying focused on Salihah. Finally, Salihah's child began to come while Imani's pain grew unbearable and she too had to take the position on the floor as her child was coming the same day as Salihah's. With no time to think, Nekteri had three of the women enter the room and light oils infused with local herbs which were in glass containers around the room; this would provide some relief from the pain of giving birth for both Salihah and Imani.

As the women were instructed to support both Salihah and Imani Nekteri delivered both babies within minutes of each other. The women who were helping had their backs to Nekteri as she delivered the babies behind the two pregnant women. In preparation for the delivery, weeks before there were several woven baskets positioned on the back wall of the annex room. Nekteri first delivered Salihah's baby and said nothing aloud as she attended to the baby, cleaned it off, and lay it in one of the baskets. While the other women helped Salihah finish her delivery, Imani began to scream followed a few moments after by the delivery of her child. Again, Nekteri collected the child and took the child over to the baskets, this time as she lay the child in the baskets the room was filled with the sounds of a baby crying.

The women assisted both Imani and Salihah through their births and moved them to the beds arranged in the annex for both of them. As they lay on the beds, Nekteri walked over a few minutes later with a baby wrapped in linen in each arm. The child in the right arm appeared to be squirming and crying for attention, while the baby in the left arm appeared still and lifeless. Nekteri stopped with the babies far enough away from the women that they could both see her with the children. Nekteri, who had begun to cry stared at Imani as if to make her read her mind. They locked eyes so long that Imani began to cry but her face resolved in a way that she understood. Imani heard the babies cry shortly after her delivery and even in a befuddled state of childbirth recalled that there were no cries after Salihah's baby was delivered. Nekteri then took the squirming baby girl over to Salihah, who too understood what had happened. While Nekteri took the lifeless body of the newborn baby over to Imani, Imani took hold of the lifeless body of a baby girl, through her tears, she grabbed Nekteri's arm and pulled her close to her. Nekteri cradled the lifeless child and lay her head on Imani's shoulder. As the women and Salihah embraced the living child and celebrated the new birth, Imani quietly, through her tears simple said to Nekteri, "Thank You."

CHAPTER ELEVEN

PLAYING CHARADES

Shortly after the birth of the children, Nekteri took the lifeless body of the child Imani held and placed her in a basket. She wrapped the body in linen and filled the basket with flowers and herbs along with issuing a prayer to Amun to receive the child into the afterlife. Nekteri also asked one of the assisting women to contact the funerary attendants to come and receive the body for proper preparation. Nekteri also took the now sleeping baby girl from Salihah and placed her in a basket that had been filled with a linen cushion filled with dried flowers and feathers and a cover of a light linen blanket. Both Salihah and Imani fell into a deep sleep.

When Nekteri finished cleaning the annex and preparing the babies the families had all arrived in the courtyard of the home of Salihah and Lateef. Nekteri ushered Lateef, Firesky, Tuhar, Anai, and Steven into the main room of their home. Nekteri explained that both Salihah and Imani gave birth at the same time but only one of the children survived childbirth. Everyone in the room wanted to ask the question of whose baby survived but decided that it was better not to question. Nekteri went on to explain that Salihah and Lateef have a new healthy baby girl with jet black wavy hair and hazel eyes. Nekteri then stepped into the annex and a few moments later brought the basket filled with the sleeping baby girl into the room. Lateef reached into the basket and cradled the baby in his arms. Firesky walked over to his father and gave a single kiss on the forehead of the child and thanked the Gods for his baby sister.

Nekteri looked at Tuhar and Anai with the same sad look she had given to Imani. Anai moved first toward Nekteri and embraced her. She knew the work that Nekteri had done today was nothing short of heroic and that she would be blessed for an eternity because of her loyalty to

King Tutankhamun and their families. Nekteri excused herself from the family gathering and returned to her home.

Salihah and Imani recovered from childbirth and thereafter both families attended the funerary for a final goodbye to what would be known as Imani's child. Imani now able to return to her lessons for reading and craftsmanship began to write and document the life of Salihah's new daughter they lovingly named Raven, because of her jet-black hair. Raven, a sweet baby, was a dark olive-skinned girl with eyes that resembled the brown-hazel hues of the sunset. Imani would create small woven tapestries depicting the life of this beautiful pure soul. Many days as Imani would journey home from Salihah's she would blow kisses to RA asking the God to deliver the kiss to Tutankhamun and hoping that he would know from the kiss that she and his heir were fine.

Meanwhile, Commander Horemheb attacked the Hittite Army using the element of surprise. Commander Horemheb devised a strategy to divide and conquer. If the now 350 Egyptian soldiers and leaders were to align to the side of the Hittite Amy, considering the Hittite Army was unaware and unprepared for an attack, we could align five rows of 70 Egyptian soldiers in full artillery to attack and kill the middle soldiers. With our flanked soldiers prepared to fight the front and rear groups of Hittites we could successfully separate the groups of soldiers and weaken their resolve. Commander Horemheb had noticed that the Hittite Generals camps were established in the middle of the soldiers and their mid group attack would further weaken their brigades by killing the Hittite leadership.

Commander Horemheb was careful to setup his Military outside and behind the tunnels, again to keep the tunnels undetected from the Hittite military and protect the surrounding villages the Kingdom of Egypt had sworn to protect. It took time for Commander Horemheb and his leaders to prepare his Military for the attack, which came at daybreak the next day. It appeared that the Hittites were nearly ready for their assault on Egypt as more of their soldier took a position and there was much activity from the Hittite leadership in communicating with the soldiers in the rear.

The Hittite soldiers were unprepared for the attack from their side, many of the soldiers had removed their body shield and helmets while others were just opening their eyes from their rest the night before. Commander Horemheb had bow-men, 40 of the soldiers, release their arrows into the crowd of Hittite soldiers which killed many soldiers and two of their Generals. He then charged in with his front infantry with Khepesh swords, daggers, and slicing axes killing as many Hittites as he could to keep them from the kingdom of Egypt. Although Commander Horemheb was successful in his initial attempt to divide and conquer the Hittite armies the fighting continued for three months as he was unaware of the additional military following the early infantry that the Hittites were sending from their country in groups of 150 to 400 at a time.

Commander Horemheb's success included saving the lives of 200 of the 400 Egyptian soldiers who joined in the fighting against the Hittite armies. The success also included saving David's life although at times during the battle Commander Horemheb saved David's life with a quick dagger to a hovering soldier. David too had to save Commander Horemheb's life on two occasions where Commander Horemheb was cornered by a Hittite general who seemed to take cover in some weeds to attack some unsuspecting Egyptian soldier at just the right time. David seen the Hittite general crouching in the weeds and grabbed a bow and arrow from the bow-men and sent an arrow straight through the chest cavity of the soldier seconds before he was to stab Commander Horemheb. At the end of the battle the tension which existed before the fighting, between Commander Horemheb and David, died away as each felt they owed the other their life.

The Army returned to the Kingdom of Egypt battered and bruised but victorious. As the military made their way out of the tunnels from Elreyah, King Tutankhamun and AY awaited at the gates of the temple facing the east gate to Elreyah. King Tutankhamun awaited his friend with great contemplation and hope. If David did not survive what would happen to Tutankhamun's secret, who would he be able to trust with the heir to his kingdom? Tutankhamun thought to himself; an heir that should have already arrived and he could not wait to see.

Commander Horemheb and David were almost the last to exit the tunnels and they approached King Tutankhamun with the news that the Hittite Army was successfully defeated but also the warning that they would likely return once they could rebuild their armies. King Tutankhamun, who was in full regalia; his blue crown which represented a time of war, his golden gem encrusted neck piece strewn across his bare chest, his freshly laundered and pressed white shendyt wrapped around his waist with the bottom laying just below the back of his knees, and his blue sash wrapped around his waist covered in front by a gold and gem-encrusted end of sash which was embossed with Osiris and Montu, the God of War. King Tutankhamun grabbed the left forearm of Commander Horemheb with his right and shook his hand with his left hand as said, "we thank the God Montu, for his protection during this war." Commander Horemheb agreed with King Tutankhamun and also thanked the God Montu and Amun for protection of the victory and protecting the people of Egypt.

In the evening, King Tutankhamun met with David before attending the celebratory dinner with Commander Horemheb, AY, and other leaders of the military. King Tutankhamun's only goal following the success of the Egypt- Hittite battle was to see Imani and his heir. Due to other assaults on Egypt and multiple miscarriages by Ankhesenamun, King Tutankhamun got to see less and less of Imani and only saw his heir four times over the next three and-a-half years.

The first time King Tutankhamun met his heir was during the wheat festival of Khuhua. King Tutankhamun arrived two days before the festival with a small caravan. King Tutankhamun arrived in the courtyard of Governor Tuhar's home with David at his side with little fanfare.

The family was not all lined up outside with Tuhar his wife and children at his side. There were not a flurry of servants awaiting their arrival to greet them and provide direction for the traveling attendants to place their gifts or where to tie up the animals, nor where the attendants would retire. Instead, David simply knocked on the door to Tuhar's home with King Tutankhamun and waited for a servant to open the door. A servant opened the door and ushered King Tutankhamun and David into the door. As they entered the home, they found Governor Tuhar and Anai sitting in chairs next to what looked like a grand bassinet with Lateef and Salihah sitting on the opposite side. Imani was leaning over the bassinet and picked up the baby girl with jet black wavy hair who was about five months old. Tutankhamun moved with as much swiftness as possible across the room to Imani, who handed him the baby and sweetly told him, "This is Raven." Raven, who was sleeping soundly instinctively, as if she knew this is was her father, cooed in her sleep and squirmed to adjust herself to his body. A single tear-drop fell down Tutankhamun's cheek and for what seemed like an eternity he simply stared at the beautiful baby that he knew he helped to create. David pushed one of the chairs close enough for Tutankhamun to sit down with the baby and as he took a seat he could not take his eyes off of her. Finally, he looked up to Imani, still with the steady stream of a tear flowing down his cheek and asked where is the other child. Solemnly, Salihah cleared her throat and said, "the child died in childbirth."

Everyone in the room watched Tutankhamun bond with the child. After he stared at her for a long period he then started rubbing her hair, it was the sweetest and most intimate moment between a father and a child that any of them had ever seen. Soon after Raven opened her eyes and even at five months old recognized King Tutankhamun. She remained still and quiet for a few moments looking intently at Tutankhamun, who for once looked like a young 14-year-old boy instead of the King of Egypt. Imani finally walked over to Tutankhamun and let him know it was time for her feeding, took the child and gave her to Salihah. Salihah retired to the back room of Tuhar's home to feed Raven, and Imani and Tutankhamun retired to her room.

Tutankhamun was speechless and just smiled at Imani with a look of true admiration. Imani, who kept her back to Tutankhamun after they entered the room, said, "My King, I do not know if it best that you be here for the festival, as I believe we will all be in grave danger including Raven."

Tutankhamun's expression went from admiration to bewilderment, confused by Imani's statement. "Why would you say that Imani, I just want to be with you and around our child as much as my crown with let me, "Tutankhamun said.

Imani responded, "if anyone suspects that you and I are together or that Raven could be your heir, my family, Lateef's family, and most importantly Raven's life could be lost." Imani continued, "I don't think for a second that AY would hesitate to murder all of us to save the kingdom and I think this festival will throw us into the hands of AY. We cannot risk that; you cannot risk that!"

Tutankhamun tried to respond to Imani telling her that he and David would protect them, but even as he said it, he didn't truly believe it.

As King Tutankhamun was mulling over in his mind how he could make it work, there was a knock at the front door of Tuhar's home. Imani moved to her door and peeked through the sliver of her room door which was in a perfect position to see any visitors coming into their home. It seemed like time slowed down and everything was moving in slow motion, for coming through the door was the kings' vizier AY and another male who appeared to be a soldier. Imani glanced at Tutankhamun who saw the grave look of concern on her face. Tutankhamun rose and approached the door to also take a peek. He immediately stepped back out of site of the cracked door. Imani carefully closed the door so that no one in the front room would hear it close. Imani scrambled to remove Tutankhamun from her room as that would tell AY that Tutankhamun and Imani were together. She had already been approached by AY asking about her pregnancy, what she did not need was to increase his curiosity. She thought quick and whispered the bath. Tutankhamun looked bewildered and confused. Imani began to lead him to the bath which had a doorway to the grand ballroom but as Tutankhamun moved, the sounds of rustling from his breastplate grew louder. The two of them stopped fearing they would be discovered, because his clothing was so noisy. Imani looked around her room to see what she could put over his breastplate to block the sounds. As Tutankhamun and Imani scrambled in the quietest way, possible Steven slipped in through the bathroom door. He looked like he was playing charades as he was trying to tell Imani and Tutankhamun, without words that he could help. Steven took his two fingers on both hands and used them to motion up and down towards the bathroom door then pointing both towards himself pointing at Tutankhamun and then towards the bathroom. It took a couple of moments for both Imani and Tutankhamun to grasp that Steven was there to save them both.

Meanwhile, AY entered the home and greeted governor Tuhar saying, "please forgive my intrusion but I am in search of King Tutankhamun." AY glanced over at David, who was standing in the corner trying not to draw attention to himself. AY turned to David and said, "Where is your King?" with as much disdain as he could muster.

David responded by calmly pointing in the direction of the ballroom, where King Tutankhamun emerged from the door.

Tutankhamun had a blank stare on his face and curtly asked AY, "What are you doing here?"

Tutankhamun was neither nice nor angry towards AY and caused his vizier to stutter over his response attempting to respond timely to Tutankhamun's request.

AY responded to King Tutankhamun saying, "My King I am here to tell you that we received notice that there has been an attack on Memphis from the sea. I am afraid we will not be able to support the additional caravan to Memphis for the festival."

King Tutankhamun responded, "Do we need to get our Military and war chariots to defend Memphis?"

AY looked around the room as if he was in mixed company and then back at King Tutankhamun who was still stone faced and responded to King Tutankhamun, "Commander Horemheb has already headed to Memphis and should subdue any danger before we arrive, we will need engineering and craftsmen support to rebuild any damage."

King Tutankhamun turned to the captivated room of friends and apologized to everyone for his festival attendance. Tuhar walked over to King Tutankhamun and put his hand on his shoulder to let him know they understood and would be available for any support should he need it. Imani and Salihah entered the room as Tuhar was biding King Tutankhamun farewell.

AY started to advance to the door then abruptly stopped, turned and asked, "Imani is that your child?"

Imani's eyes grew slightly larger in an instance asking herself did he know, but gathered herself and said, "AY my child died during childbirth, this is their child," as Imani waved her hand in the direction of Salihah and Lateef.

AY glanced around the room at each person including King Tutankhamun, who again was stone-faced, settled on Lateef and slightly bowed his head. AY, King Tutankhamun, and David exited the home of Tuhar and returned to Egypt.

King Tutankhamun would not see Raven again for two years. Tutankhamun's travels to Memphis turned out to be more damaging than AY originally described. King Tutankhamun returned to the area when he was 16 years old to participate in the Opet Festival. During the festival, all communities were invited to participate and give thanks and gifts to the gods along with asking questions of the Gods with answers given to the priest who would then give answers to the people. As King Tutankhamun, a king of the people walked through the Temple at Luxor a two-year-old Raven spotted the king and went barreling from the hand of Salihah toward King Tutankhamun. If it were not for the Kings recognition of the raven-haired girl, she would have been admonished along with her family. Tutankhamun caught a glimpse of her running towards him with her parents running at top speed behind her, couched down, opened his arms and received Raven's hug. Raven, ever so innocently held onto the King's neck for dear life. The actions by Raven and the response from King Tutankhamun was so rare that across the quadrant AY turned and watched the exchange while Ankhesenamun caught the hug of Raven to Tutankhamun from the third floor of the temple.

Finally, Salihah and Lateef, along with Firesky who was so shocked his sister would defy all tradition in that way caught up to Raven and King Tutankhamun. He looked around at all of the people watching his sister be inappropriate with the King. He just knew the Army would be there soon to kill them. Lateef apologized to the king for Raven's behavior and attempted to pull Raven from the King. King Tutankhamun motioned with his hand that her actions were acceptable to him and still crouched to the ground began to ask Raven how she was doing. Tutankhamun who was crouching with a cane got battered with questions from the inquisitive two-year-old.

"Why do you have a cane? What is this you have around your neck, as she touched his breastplate, can I stay with you? Do you like my hair?" Raven said without seeming to take a breath.

King Tutankhamun just laughed and told Raven, "You are going to have to come visit me more often if you have so many questions, and yes I love your hair."

Raven seemed to be satisfied with the King's answer, took Salihah's hand and waved goodbye to the King and walked away with her family. King Tutankhamun seemed oblivious to all of the eyes watching his exchange with his little girl. He stared at her for a few moments and then continued his walk through the Opet Festival.

After the Opet Festival, King Tutankhamun saw Raven again when she was almost four years old. Over the previous three years, Imani and Tutankhamun had exchanged more than 100 letters. Tutankhamun had shared his run-in with Raven at the Opet Festival and how much he loved seeing her run to his arms as if she had seen him every day of her life. Imani wrote back and told Tutankhamun that Raven shared her experience and would tell her that she just loved the king. Since that time Raven had learned so much and grown into a beautiful girl that was full of spirit and love. Imani told Tutankhamun how proud she was to have shared their child together. She also asked that Tutankhamun come back to visit her at least one more time.

CHAPTER TWELVE

ONE OF THE MOST STRATEGIC PEOPLE

King Tutankhamun decided to take time away from the kingdom to visit the local communities surrounding Egypt, which he had not done in more than three years. The Kingdom had been at peace for three years and it was time to reconnect with the leaders that supported the Kingdom of Egypt. David, who was now a lieutenant in the Amy, continued to visit Khuhua over the past three years and grew to know Raven and stay close with Tuhar, Lateef, Imani and all of the kids. David who was now 17 years old decided that his time would be spent teaching Steven, Firesky, Aaron, Apollo, and even Miriam who acted more like a boy than a girl, some military strategies they could use in their games. King Tutankhamun requested David's presence to plan his visits.

On the day King Tutankhamun requested David's presence David was just returning from surveying the tunnels entrances and exits to confirm there was sufficient foliage to ensure the tunnels remained undetected from their enemies. Before seeing King Tutankhamun, David visited the office of AY to report the status of the tunnels. AY asked David to sit with him as he wanted to inquire about the fortification of the tunnels and a few other issues that gave him concern. AY asked David to tell him about each of the cities connected to the tunnels. David went in a litany of details about each city; Khuhua which was known for its massive wheat harvest along with other agriculture that thrived on silt: wet and nutrient-rich soil. Khuhua was the city most affected by the inundation flooding and had the greatest acreage of wheat harvesting land. Elreyah was known for the largest harvest of grapes for wine production and supplied more wine to the kingdom than any other community. Bahariya produces more barley and beer than any other community surrounding Egypt. Sakka, the community closest to the Red Sea was a fishing community and traded fish with all other communities, they were blessed with the Gods of the water and gave more fish to Egypt as unto the Gods. Farafra being close to El Fayum and farthest away from the Nile were irrigation specialists and provided clean water from the Springs outside of El Fayum and irrigation skills to all of the surrounding communities. All of these communities not only provided agricultural goods to Egypt, but they also supported Egypt's efforts to maintain thier military strength.

AY then asked David about the governmental structure of each of the cities and what he knew about each one. David, having no reason to hold back information from the Vizier, again he informed AY about each governor and their families and how their leaders were very supportive of King Tutankhamun and his efforts to remain in peace. The outreach that you made King Tutankhamun perform beginning when he was 9 or 10 was the greatest connection to the communities Egypt has experienced. AY then asked David about what happened to Imani's baby. David, who normally controlled his emotions, shifted from a controlled army lieutenant to an uncomfortable child. David answered AY by timidly saying, "You were in the room with King Tutankhamun and me when Imani expressed that her baby died in childbirth. Why are you asking me now?"

AY responded, "I saw the child with the raven colored hair run up to King Tutankhamun at the Opet Festival, and their embrace allowed me to see the resemblance between that child and our King." David told AY to ask King Tutankhamun his thoughts about the child and coldly stated, "I told you everything I know, the child is dead." As David left AY's office, he watched him slowly walk to his office window which faced the east stables and military annex.

David left AY's office and went to King Tutankhamun's living quarters located in the northeastern quadrant of the palace. David knocked on the door to Tutankhamun's quarters and entered the side annex to the left of the front door into King Tutankhamun offices. King

Tutankhamun was standing at the floor to ceiling window of his office when David entered. King Tutankhamun greeted David and started telling him his thoughts about traveling to each of the communities in the region over the next three months. He thought it a great idea to keep Khuhua as the last stop in the caravan and give him no less than three days with Imani. King Tutankhamun stopped his rambling when he saw his friend was not paying attention and asked David what was happening to make him ignore his instructions.

David shared with King Tutankhamun his encounter with AY about the surrounding communities. David told King Tutankhamun that after telling AY about the communities and their support, he asked about Imani and the baby. David went on to tell Tutankhamun that he felt AY did not believe the baby was dead and that Raven was your heir and added that he didn't believe AY would leave this alone. Since you and Ankhesenamun have had two children who have died, I believe he feels the fate of the kingdom and his future rest solely on Raven's life. "What do you want me to do, Tutankhamun," David asked boldly.

King Tutankhamun, who was one of the most strategic people David knew, thought deeply about what he would do. David could see when King Tutankhamun came to a resolve for what to do next. "David, please prepare the caravans with gifts, food, and attendants, enough for the next 30 days. We will spend five days each at Elreyah, Farafra, Bahariya, and Sakka and spend the last ten days in Khuhua. Please send a notification to each of these governors so that they may prepare for a grand ball to include all officials and noble persons. We will leave in five days," King Tutankhamun responded. David asked Tutankhamun to explain how to avoid the suspicions of AY and the priests. Tutankhamun told David, "To ask AY to join us on our journeys to each of the cities. AY does not have the stamina of a young man and does not enjoy meeting people in the community, let's just see how long he lasts on our journey to connect with the people." David left King Tutankhamun's presence and executed his orders. He decided he would visit Khuhua himself to inform Tuhar and Imani of King Tutankhamun's plans. Both Tuhar and Imani became excited about Tutankhamun's visit, and Tuhar decided to implement a plan of his own to ensure Imani would have time alone for the full ten days even if AY decided to stay.

As David was leaving Tuhar's home, he spotted Firesky, Steven, and their friends playing in the streets. David approached the friends and showed them how to appear to be one person, like the Hittite Armies and then ambush their enemies. They put the tallest and widest child in front of the group; then every other child was to line up with their arms bent at the elbows touching the person in front of them. By using this strategy, they could come upon an enemy as one person then as they grew closer to the enemy everyone could come out and ambush or capture their enemy. As long as each person knew the part they played in the strategy, it would always work to overcome their enemy. After sharing the strategy game with the kids, David returned to the kingdom.

After five days, the caravan set out for the farthest community which was Sakka located next to the Red Sea and the farthest from the Kingdom. King Tutankhamun fulfilled his promise to celebrate with each of the communities starting with Sakka and ending in Khuhua. AY traveled as far as Farafra and grew tired of shaking hands with every official in the governing party, after that he returned to Egypt and gave King Tutankhamun his blessing for the remainder of his journey. On the 21st day, King Tutankhamun arrived in Khuhua to great fanfare and praise from the local community. King Tutankhamun had baskets of gifts to give to the Governor who in-turn asked that Tutankhamun's servants take their gifts, with King Tutankhamun's blessing, to the city square where all in the community may partake of the blessings bestowed by the king. Thereafter, Tuhar invited King Tutankhamun and David into his home and shared his plans for King Tutankhamun and Imani for the next ten days. Governor Tuhar arranged for King Tutankhamun and Imani to reside in the second home Tuhar owned which was located just outside of the city of Khuhua.

For security, there was a tunnel below Tuhar's current home that would allow the two of them to access the home without fear of being spotted within the community.

King Tutankhamun was overwhelmed by Tuhar's generosity and asked what he could do for the community of Khuhua to repay him. Governor Tuhar with his wife Anai at his side explained to King Tutankhamun that they were grateful for the child Raven who had been a blessing to the family. They went on to explain how the Kings willingness to allow them to keep the child in the community instead of the King taking the child to live with him in the palace was more than any other gift the King could offer. The Kings love for their daughter has not wavered, and they respected the Kings dedication. Tutankhamun, who was choked up with emotion, simply embraced Tuhar and then Anai and said thank you for your love. Tuhar then led Tutankhamun through the secret tunnel where Imani was already preparing a small feast for just she and her king.

For the first five days of King Tutankhamun's visit, he and Imani would leave their private space to visit the local leaders first then the home of Lateef and Salihah to spend time with Raven. Raven was full of energy and questions each time she saw King Tutankhamun. She asked him why he always wore white, why can't girls go to school? Why can't you come and live here with us? Why are my eyes like Imani's and yours are not? Tutankhamun would do his best to be attentive and give Raven a response to everything she asked. Eventually, Salihah would rescue Tutankhamun to either feed Raven or put her to bed. Before Raven would willingly go with her mother Salihah, she would ask Tutankhamun if he would return with Imani the next day. For the duration of his stay he told Raven he would be back to see her the next day.

On the ninth day of his visit, King Tutankhamun sat down in the main room with Lateef and Salihah and talked with Firesky and Steven about being men and protecting the city of Khuhua. King Tutankhamun told the boys that he was younger than them when he became the ruler of Egypt. He told them sometimes the impossible thing to do was just what they were designed to do. Never be afraid to walk in your destiny, and you will always be successful. My father, Akhenaten told me he was never in-line to be king, but it was his destiny. Both Steven and Firesky were super excited to be talking to King Tutankhamun and only partially listened to his message. King Tutankhamun knew them by name, and they were only too excited to accept that they were now best friends with the King.

CHAPTER THIRTEEN

WHO CALLED YOU FROM INSIDE THE HOUSE

On the last day of King Tutankhamun's visit, he and Imani went to the wheat fields to lay together as they had done at the time they confessed their love for each other. As they lay together on the outside of Khuhua they suddenly heard lots of commotion that seemed to be coming from the city streets. Tutankhamun and Imani arose to see smoke rising from the city square, they looked at each other and could only think of Raven. The two made their way through the wheat fields and came out between the same houses that David had found Imani and Steven when he had come to save them from AY. The two of them passed through the houses into the square and turned to their right toward Tuhar's home. The only thing they could see was a billow of smoke that was so dense they could not tell if there were any people behind the smoke.

King Tutankhamun yelled out for David, who responded from what seemed like the center of the billow of smoke. David yelled out," the fire was set deliberately as a distraction, I need water to put it out." Within a few minutes, the fire that had been set ablaze in a basket in the middle of the street was doused with water, and the smoke subsided. Bewildered citizens of Khuhua were wandering the streets asking if everyone was alright. Imani left King Tutankhamun's side and went to Lateef and Salihah home looking for Raven. Salihah who had come outside when the smoke started to billow searched her home, the rear of her home and then started frantically going from house to house screaming Raven's name praying to RA that Raven would respond to her calls. Salihah came to the house of Miriam who was outside standing like a statute, looking at the billow of smoke. Salihah grabbed Miriam by the shoulders and started shaking her to break her from her spell. "Did you see her; did you see who took her?" Salihah asked almost in a scream.

Miriam slowly and growing louder, like a crescendo said, "It was him! It was the servant in Tuhar's home! He took Raven in the tunnels! It was him!" Imani rushed over to Miriam, who had begun to cry uncontrollably, and embraced her and calmed her down.

King Tutankhamun could not contain his anger he instructed David to grab all attendants and bring Raven back. Do not kill the servant who took her, instead, I want him held in the chambers on his knees tied to a pole awaiting my return. All the smoke had cleared from the city, and Tuhar and family were able to gather themselves and meet with King Tutankhamun to understand what happened. Tutankhamun asked Tuhar and family to console Lateef and Salihah during this difficult time. He assured them he would do all in his power to bring Raven back to their care.

Firesky who had watched and listened to King Tutankhamun was full of rage and felt there was more to this issue. He turned around and walked up to a weeping Miriam to understand exactly what happened. Firesky snapped at Miriam with more anger directed at her than he intended. He yelled, "Tell me everything; you know what happened. That is my sister, tell me." Firesky through his anger reluctantly started crying and with each word, he cried harder and yelled louder. Miriam, started taking deep breaths to slow down her crying and control her words. Although her voice remained shaky, she told Firesky that she was sitting on the tree stump outside of my house staring at the trees just past Governor Tuhar's courtyard. This was not unusual as she was often caught gazing while on that stump in front of her family's home. There was a servant who had been sitting outside of the courtyard all morning. He looked like he was waiting for instructions for gathering the harvest. I thought it was crazy that he was sitting outside of Governor Tuhar's home as no one usually waits there for harvesting. Raven was outside playing with her toys in Lateef and Salihah's courtyard. Salihah looked like someone called her from inside her house, and she got up and went inside. Then the servant took a basket full of leaves and twigs and started the fire in a couple of seconds. Before the smoke billowed, I saw another man with a blue sash around his waist walk up behind him then turn around and run toward the tunnels. I saw the servant run over to Raven pick her up and put a linen cloth over her mouth and run toward the tunnels.

"I am so sorry I didn't scream or something else to bring attention to the man, but I was just frozen to this spot," Miriam stated starting to cry again. "I am so sorry, I am so sorry, I am so sorry, "Miriam repeated to Firesky, while Imani continued to console her. Firesky walked over to his home and asked his mother in a calm voice, "Who called you from inside the house, what did they say who did they sound like?" Salihah responded, "I don't know, I heard someone call me from inside and I left Raven out here for just a second to see who it was." Salihah began to cry again, as she felt that Raven was gone because of her.

Hours passed and night fell on Khuhua as the city was calmer yet still in chaos because of the kidnapping of Raven. Everyone in the community knew the girl with the hazel eyes and jet black wavy hair which was now down to the middle of her back who asked everyone she met a barrage of questions. Everyone loved Raven and protected her like she was their own daughter. How was it that an entire community could not protect their beloved? King Tutankhamun questioned every attendant he had about this servant who took Raven. When each was asked no one knew this servant and told the same story that he had just come to Khuhua that morning. He had the mark of the Kingdom, so there was no reason to be suspicious of him, they were just unfamiliar with him. At the time of the kidnapping, all servants were preparing for the next day's departure and spent time attending to the animals or inside Tuhar's home laundering and preparing food for the journey home.

King Tutankhamun decided to leave that night to convene with David and the search party. David had to have found the kidnapper and Raven by then, as it was hours since David left to discover the truth. As King Tutankhamun had mixed emotions about leaving Imani, Imani made it easier for the King. You have to go and find our child; this is the only thing that is important. That was the first time in four years he heard Imani refer to Raven as their child out loud it gave him, even more, determination to find Raven and bring her back to Khuhua. King Tutankhamun kissed Imani on the forehead and bid farewell to the others including a wink at both Firesky and Steven who received the wink as their duty to help wherever they could.

Meanwhile, when David and the attendants each on their own horse got to the tunnels, which seemed like only minutes after the kidnapper went through the tunnels, he saw a man on a horse running full speed and was about 6 kilometers from the entrance. David thought he saw a second horse in front of the first man he saw, but the distance and movement made it almost impossible for him to know definitively. David took off knowing he needed to make up time before Raven was lost forever. With the width of the tunnels being 1.8 meters wide by 3 meters high David and the attendants would be able to gain top speed on the horses down the 10-

kilometer tunnel.

David made it out of the tunnels and slowed the horses to a trot to survey the area surrounding the entrance of the tunnels David was the regular surveyor of the tunnels and was very familiar with the environment as the tunnels ran south to north from Khuhua to the Kingdom and the proximity to the Nile at the entrance of the tunnel was a little farther than Khuhua's distance from the Nile by about 3 kilometers. The entrance to the tunnel was surrounded by date trees and other tall grasses. The land leading to the Kingdom was a mix of sandy soil with patches of green foliage. The one advantage David had on other travelers is that he knew the direction of the wind and how the sandy soil responded as travelers moved through the area. The pathway to the Kingdom was northwest of the tunnel entrance, but David noticed the sand trails in the sand appeared to move northeast. This would mean that the kidnappers were traveling away from the Kingdom. Did that mean this was an act of war on the Kingdom perhaps by the Hittites or another enemy?

David took a moment to think of what was in the Northeast. The only communities in the northeast that David was aware of was the Setum settlement, but the people who lived there were more nomads rather than a true community at the mouth of the Red Sea. Why would they go that way, instead of going to the Kingdom, unless they were an enemy? Or perhaps, like the fire started to make a smoke diversion, they were trying to look like an enemy. David asked the attendants traveling with him did any of them know the servant who took Raven? Only two of the attendants saw the servant, and neither of them recognized them. David followed up his question by asking them did the servant look foreign? One of the attendants told David that the servant had the same branding they had as an Egyptian servant. The servant pulled up his long-sleeved linen tunic on his right arm to reveal a symbol of wheat stalks held together by bird talons that was about 2 x 2 tenths of a cubit to the right of his elbow. I saw the engraving on him, because unlike the rest of us he was wearing a short-sleeved tunic. The attendant continued to tell David that there was another man who wore a royal sash of blue around his waist with the King's emblem of a snake at the base of the blue gems.

David brought the horses to a complete stop to contemplate the information he received from the attendants. He asked himself, why would they be traveling northeast, perhaps they were traveling to the Temple of Aten located at the mouth of the Delta. The only person who ever visited this temple was AY and from David's understanding this Temple that one of the most beautiful in the world built by King Tutankhamun's mother/aunt Smenkhkara during her reign as pharaoh before Tutankhamun and was supposed to be abandoned. The only ones who knew about the abandoned Temple were the scribes, craftsman, Commander Horemheb, and AY. The reason David knew about the temple was due to his time spent with King Tutankhamun during the Ethiopian raid where they were forced to learn about the history of the Kingdom, their various Temples, and Egypt's enemies. Following those lessons, David continued his lessons of history as he advanced within Egyptian military. David dismounted his horse and looked out at the horizon where the sun was beginning to descend, and nightfall would soon be upon them. He paced as he thought about how to find the child, and how to survey two places at once to ensure they found the child alive.

David considered the attendants he had brought with him, two were skilled with animals, one was a baker, while the other was a blacksmith and skilled in the art of hand to hand combat as he had trained Egyptian soldier how to use the instruments he created or crafted to give Egyptian soldiers an advantage in battle. David tore off a piece of his red sash which showed a symbol which represented his military ranking as a lieutenant and gave it to one of the attendant skilled as a herdsman. David instructed the herdsman and baker to travel to the kingdom request an audience with Commander Horemheb and present the sash to him. Tell him that someone has declared war on the Kingdom by kidnapping a child of one of the governing leaders controlled by the Kingdom of Egypt. Tell

Commander Horemheb that I have traveled to the Temple of Aten at the mouth of the Delta. Also, tell him to tell none of the priest or Vizier of his location, but send military support to the region. David mounted his horse and with the blacksmith took off for the Temple of Aten. The attendants traveled northwest to the Kingdom to execute David's orders and arrived at the Kingdom just as the sun disappeared from the horizon.

CHAPTER FOURTEEN

TELL ME THE TRUTH!

As King Tutankhamun left for the Kingdom, Firesky went to his family's courtyard and cried as he was feeling hopeless and useless. He was supposed to protect his sister from danger, he didn't have the power to make the change in his community like he and Stevens parent's, but the one thing he could do was protect his sister. Firesky was so lost in thought that he did not realize that Steven had entered the courtyard and sat beside him. Firesky looked up into the face of Steven to see him looking like he wanted to tell him something. Steven was round-faced, had dark olive skin, and hazel eyes like Raven's. That was one of the reasons Firesky liked Steven so much; he always reminded him of his sweet-faced sister. Firesky noticed that Steven was crying because his eyes were red and looked like the inside of a ripe freshly cut fig. Firesky asked, "Other than my sister being kidnapped, is there something else wrong?" Steven whispered just loud enough for Firesky to hear, "you need to ask for the truth!" Firesky watched his best friend whisper his command and then start crying again.

Firesky, surprised by Steven's command, knew his friend was not as dramatic as Aaron and Apollo. Firesky also knew that Steven was not a liar, but was confused by what Steven had just said. Firesky took a second to respond, and then asked Steven, "Ask Who for What truth?" Steven steadied himself and stopped crying, looked Firesky in the eyes and told him, "There is another story about Raven that you need to ask your parents about, this is the key you need to know how to help your sister." Firesky stared at Steven for a few seconds, then ran into his house yelling for his Mom, whom he found in the main room where she sat with his father and Imani. Firesky, talking loud enough for Steven to hear him from the courtyard, "Tell me the TRUTH! What don't I know about Raven?" Firesky did not intend to yell at his parents, but he was overcome by his emotions, and the words came out uncontrollably. Firesky was sad, angry, confused, lost, hopeless, helpless, and anxious all at the same time; he was capable of anything at this moment.

Lateef, Salihah, and Imani all sat stunned at the question Firesky blurted out to them. Lateef, who towered over the 10-year-old Firesky standing just over 2 meters tall to Firesky's 1 ½ meters tall walked over to Firesky knelt to the floor and embraced his son. Lateef was a man who never raised his voice as his stature, and deep voice was more than sufficient to command authority. Lateef released a visibly upset Firesky and walked him over to the seat next to Imani. Lateef looked at Imani and told her this was her decision and that both he and Salihah would support her in every way. Firesky grew more upset as he heard his father pass responsibility to the neighbor and he thought he would never get the truth. As Firesky started to speak Imani interrupted him by telling him, "Raven is your sister, Salihah is her mother, Lateef is her father, and I too am her Mother, and our great King Tutankhamun is her father too."

Firesky looked at Imani with a dazed and confused look, and said in a lower tone than he had been speaking, "What do you mean, how can she have two mothers and two fathers." As Firesky was speaking a thin Steven walked into to the main room looking almost sickly from all of his crying and sat next to Firesky. Imani shifted to face Firesky and began to explain that she loved King Tutankhamun with all of her heart and through their love she became pregnant at the same time that Salihah, his mom became pregnant. In the midst of the pregnancy AY, the kings' vizier attempted to kill both herself and Steven when he discovered the child I was carrying was the only heir to the Kingdom of Egypt. Since Salihah and I were such good friends and you and Steven were the best of friends we asked that your mom and dad take the child as their own for her protection. When it came time to deliver the babies, we discovered that the baby Salihah was carrying had died, and so I would give her Raven with the hope that they would always allow me and my family to share in the child growing up. We decided not to tell you, Firesky, along with anyone else in the community to protect this wonderful city of ours. We knew that you would love and protect Raven as your own and she would have an amazing family to grow up with. Now I believe Raven's kidnapping is AY's doing as he was the only one who suspected that Raven was my child instead of believing that my child died in childbirth.

When Imani finished explaining the story of Raven, he sat bewildered at the incredible story, but being 10 years old and having crafted extraordinary stories like this before, albeit make-believe, he was able to accept it. Firesky responded to Imani in a concerned voice, "What do we do now?" Firesky changed from an angry kid to a young man ready to take on the world. Imani responded, "We wait for King Tutankhamun to find Raven and bring her home."

Firesky looked at each of them individually around the room, "Is that ALL we are going to do? No one is going to go after this mad-man who thinks they can just take our sister like a rag doll? This is crazy if you all are not going to do anything, I WILL!" Firesky rose from his seat, not waiting for anyone to respond, looked at Steven as if to tell him let's go and they walked out the front door.

Steven pulled on Firesky's hand as soon as they crossed the threshold on the outside of the front door. Steven looked at Firesky and told him, "I think you took King Tutankhamun's speech a little too seriously today, WHAT DO YOU THINK WE CAN DO? Raven is just as important to me as she is to you, although she asks waaaay too many question's, but other than that I love her and want her to come back to. But please remember we are just kids with NOOOO POWER." Steven stressed that they have no power with his words, voice, and his face to make sure Firesky understood.

Firesky responded like he never heard anything that Steven said, "Hey Steven do you remember when Aaron and Apollo had their magic stage, do you think they still have some of that disappearing powder and those toy things that make a really loud sound that their mother hates with a passion?"

Steven shrugged his shoulders and said, "I don't know, why don't you ask them, they're coming this way."

Aaron and Apollo were walking over to Firesky with lanterns no one else in the village had. Their dad was a master craftsman and engineer for Egypt and would always come home with something the Kingdom rejected, so Aaron and Apollo would play their two and one games with their dad. You would think after ten years their dad would be able to tell the twins apart from each other, but since their dad was always traveling, I guess by the time he got back home he forgets who is who. Aaron and Apollo love it because they get all kinds of stuff they can use to freak out the community and we all get to have a great time. The lantern they were carrying looked like a birdcage with a fire inside. Although the castle used oil lanterns to light the pathways in the kingdom their dad made a lantern that no one would have to refill with oil and it was brighter than the old lanterns. The priest, who were in charge of approving new engineering projects told their dad that they didn't like that it was so bright and was afraid people in the kingdom would go blind because it was too bright. The priests didn't like it because it would help people to see how mean they were. As Aaron and Apollo approached, Firesky asked them why they were out so late. Aaron snorted his response, "My mom is freaking out about Raven's kidnapping and had to take a nap. We figured we could be more useful over here." Apollo nodded sheepishly in agreement with Aaron. Apollo looked from Steven to Firesky, "so what's the plan?"

Steven started shaking his head and said, "there is no plan, we're just morning Raven's disappearance." Aaron quirked his lips to his right side looking at Steven, then looked at Firesky, "look guys I know you're doing something, because you're a doer like us. When we were playing hide and seek with Raven and you thought she was gone too long you stopped the game to make sure you could find her. When we were harvesting the melons and she was supposed to be sitting still waiting for you to finish, you looked up and couldn't see her on the bench you dropped all of the melons you had cut from the vine to go look for Raven, even though she had just crawled under the bench to find her colors she had dropped. There is no way you are going to simply sit by and wait for anyone to find your sister for you." Firesky nodded in agreement with their statements and closed his eyes as if to muster the courage to push forward with his idea.

Firesky opened his eyes and true to his name he appeared to have fire coming from his eyes, his resolve was settled he was going to save his sister. He didn't care if Raven was his birth sister or that his parents hadn't told him the full truth about the situation, all Firesky cared about was, that the little round-faced, hazel eyed, raven haired, smart, question filled, beautiful sister needed him to come save her.

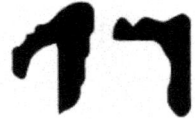

CHAPTER FIFTEEN

WHAT HAPPENS AFTER...

Firesky and his friends sat in the courtyard of his home contemplating the plan to save Raven. Firesky told his friends, "We have no idea where Raven is, we have no idea who specifically took her, and we have no way to get to where she is."

Steven stated the obvious, "How are we going to save Raven when we don't know anything?"

Firesky interrupted Steven, "I believe she is at the kingdom, because AY would not risk everything and not have her close enough for him to control. That is where we are going! We need a way to get there and Aaron we are going to need some things that will get us in and out without being caught."

Aaron looked at Apollo and nodded his head, as if to confirm they both agreed, like they could read each other's mind. They then began to talk amongst themselves about what tools they could use on the journey. The twins were infamous in their community for finding creative ways to wreak havoc while simultaneously having a great time with their friends.

As Firesky was talking to his friends in the courtyard, he failed to notice that his father was standing at the threshold of the door to the courtyard, listening to his exchange. Firesky turned to speak to Miriam and caught a glimpse of his father in his peripheral vision. Firesky made eye contact with his father and tried to read his face to determine if he was angry.

Lateef, with the look of contemplation, stepped into the courtyard, and the voices of the friends fell silent. The light from the moon seemed to get brighter as Firesky was able to see every inflection on his father face.

"Are you all trying to get to Egypt to rescue Raven?" Lateef asked the group staring fixedly on Firesky.

Steven responded first, "Sir, we are thinking about how it could be possible to save Raven, but if you want us to wait for King Tutankhamun to return with her, we would take your advice." Steven, was not ready to take on the kingdom, he wanted to save Raven, but wished they had more adult supervision and everyone's permission. He truly felt this was a mission better served with adults who had the power and authority to work together to save Raven.

"Yes Sir, we are trying to get to Egypt to rescue Raven, we can't wait for AY to kill her without any of us ever knowing the truth," replied Firesky who did not acknowledge Stevens response.

"Well, we better get working on a plan and get you all some help!" Lateef said blankly, turned and went back into the house.

Firesky and Steven were both speechless, did his father just say he would help them go on a journey to save his sister who was being held captive by the King's Vizier? The boys looked at each other as if to confirm they both heard the same thing. Steven silently nodded as if to answer Firesky's unspoken question. While Aaron and Apollo, not seeming to be surprised by the bombshell Firesky's dad just dropped, continued discussing the tools they would need.

Miriam broke the silence, "I will be right back with my dresses!" she arose and walked out of the courtyard towards her home.

Firesky and Steven followed her with their eyes until they were interrupted by Lateef, Salihah, and Imani crossing the threshold of the door and joining the kids in the courtyard. Firesky looked up at his mother to see the pained look on her face. His determination rising while his shock diminished from his father's willingness to help.

"I will be the voice of reason, this is crazy and we should let King Tutankhamun find

Raven," Imani said in a tone that sounded more like a question than a convicting statement.

Steven began to respond, "I agree…" but was interrupted by Firesky.

"Imani, if what you said was correct, that AY wants to kill my sister then King Tutankhamun will have a really hard time getting the support he needs to save her. You say that you gave Raven to my mom and dad to keep her a secret from the kingdom, since she is the only rightful heir to the throne of Egypt. You also said that AY didn't believe you when you told him that Raven is not the child of you and King Tutankhamun, and Steven told me that the only person who knows other than you, my mom and dad and your mom and dad is lieutenant David. If this is true tell me how is King Tutankhamun going to be able to save her without someone asking why he cares about one child?" Firesky said with building conviction and courage in his voice.

Firesky looked from Imani to his mom and

then his dad, searching for a response they could not give to him. He continued to speak, "I know I am only a child and have no authority in the Kingdom of Egypt, but I also know my sister is the victim of a kidnapping and she does not deserve to die. My friends and I are ready to do whatever it takes to find her and bring her home. If it was AY who took Raven, then he has her close to him and we have to find a way to get to her soon. King Tutankhamun has too much to lose if they discover that Raven is his child. Let us try!"

Lateef grabbed the shoulders of his son, stood behind him facing the kids, his wife and Imani and told them, "We will help you bring Raven home!"

As if to encourage Salihah and Imani to agree Lateef looked intently at both of them until they both shook their heads in agreement to helping Firesky and friends take on the kingdom to save one child, their child. Lateef went on to explain that there was a caravan of youth heading to the Kingdom in the morning. The youth would be taking wheat, art, and other products to trader's row to trade and sell to the citizens who live in and around the kingdom. He suggested putting a plan together overnight so the kids would get on the caravan the next morning. The kids would have until the sunset to find Raven and get back on the caravan. If the sun were to set and they did not have Raven, they would be stuck in the kingdom and subject to being caught by the Egyptian guards.

As Lateef completed his idea, Miriam was walking back into the courtyard with her grandfather Samuel whom she lived with. He was a Nubian prince who took refuge in Khuhua more than twenty years' prior after escaping with his wife and children from war that had been taking place in his home for many years. Samuel shared that he would be driving the caravan tomorrow and would be happy to do his part to rescue the child. Samuel, who had previously worked with the Kingdom of Egypt as the chief architect also brought a copy of the plans of all of the inside tunnels of the kingdom. He had designed them to help the attendants assist the King and his court without being seen or interrupting their intimate conversations. The inside tunnels would get the kids anywhere in the kingdom without being seen, but the only challenge would be to get from corridor to corridor. The Temple was designed with no interruption of RA and his power of the sun. So there will be several entry and exit ways from one corridor to the next corridor located in the next building tunnel.

Everyone surveyed the map of King Tutankhamun's temple which was abandon when his father moved the capital of Egypt from Thebes to the City of Amarna for a period of 10 years. The capital city of Thebes was restored when Akhenaten died and Tutankhamun became Pharaoh. At which time the restoration and expansion of this temple of Tutankhamun in Thebes was completed. The plans shared by Samuel showed a massive outline of the property including the stone wall which surrounded the temple along with the courtyard entrance that was flanked by two obelisks. Behind the obelisks were stairs leading up to the entrance of the grand hall which was to the right of the entryway to the temple. An open courtyard spanned the inner section of the temple, one could stand at the entryway of the temple and see straight to the back of the temple wall. The entryway and the courtyard looked large enough to fit two chariots side by side into the front and through the courtyard. The plans showed additional open courtyards located on the back side of each of the side buildings while the back of the side buildings was capped with what resembled an auditorium which spanned the width of the two side buildings and the middle courtyard. The front of the temple included the courtyard that looked large enough to fit over 100 chariots with men in them.

The plans showed that the rectangular buildings were a maze of living quarters and they could see the narrow lines on the plans that only Samuel understood were the corridors in the walls where attendants could travel to assist the king and queens along with their staff and guests. Samuel pointed to several points on the plans that showed the gap between the corridors where the kids would have to find ways to move undetected from one corridor exit to the other corridor entrance.

As Samuel finished explaining several points in the temple of Tutankhamun floor plan Lateef opened his plans of the temple showing the water mains in the temple. Lateef was in charge of maintaining the water supply and water flow in all of Egypt including the water supplies in Khuhua. As the plans were overlaid on the architectural floor plan it showed at the points where the corridors ended there was a water well juncture. The kids may be able to use the water wells in some way to distract others in the temples to freely move from corridor to corridor.

Aaron and Apollo looked at each other, again as if they could read each other's mind. In the darkness Apollo picked up the lantern and told the group that they would soon return with the tools for this journey. Aaron, who was closer to Firesky, grabbed Firesky's arm and looked him square in the eyes and told him, "We are going to save your sister! Just be ready for what happens after she is saved."

Firesky nodded at Aaron, then the twins turned and left the courtyard heading toward their home. Firesky briefly contemplated Aaron's words: "Just be ready for what happens after she is saved." He didn't think Aaron was trying to discourage them from this adventure, but it was a curious statement as Firesky never thought about what could happen after. Once Raven was home that would be the end of the story and they could all go back to living as normal, Right? Firesky shook his head and returned to the discussion regarding the Temple of Tutankhamun's plans that lay on the courtyard table.

16

ANYONE LOOKING FOR HER

The rest of the night was spent speculating where Raven could be in the temple. She would need to be in an area of the temple where she could be undetected by most of the staff and anyone in Tutankhamun's court especially King Tutankhamun himself. Samuel shared that he thought she could be in only one of two places where no one in King Tutankhamun's court would go. The first idea was in the priest's temple, which was adjacent to the main quarters and closest to the exit going south to the temple at Karnack. The priest temple was a square image on Samuels architectural plans, as there was another plan which displayed the full floor plan of the priest's temple. Samuel went on to explain that because of the strained relationship between Akhenaten, King Tutankhamun's father and the priests, when the capital of Egypt was restored in Thebes the priests made the boy king sign a decree that no one other than the priests could freely enter and exit the priest's temples. Because of this decree, it would be easy to hide a child in the priest temple. Samuel did not look convinced that this was where the child was, as the priests and priestesses where not fond of keeping children in their presence unless it was specific to their purposes.

Salihah responded to Samuels unspoken concern, "Are you not convinced Raven is there?

Samuel, obviously contemplating something in his head, shook his head and said, "I know this is an option, particularly if AY has paid the priest to harbor the child, but I have worked with the priests who have little patience for people. Their focus is on the God's and anyone who interferes with their ability to hear from the God's and translate that to the King is more of an irritant than a help." Samuel sighed and continued; "I have seen the priests in action during the day, they are very focused on their routines, interrupting that with a young child would send them into a frenzy. So to answer your question, Salihah, unless there is an event that involves girls taking place tomorrow, I do not see the child being with the priests."

"The alternative location where Raven could be is the queens second quarters. Queen Ankhesenamun resides on right side of the temple in the rear quarters closest to the auditorium. She originally had quarters on the left side of the temple, close to King Tutankhamun's quarters." Samuel pointed to the areas on the floor plans where Queen Ankhesenamuns' quarters were on the right side of the temple, then pointed to the original Queens quarters located on the left rear section of the temple. Samuel also pointed to King Tutankhamun's quarters which appeared to be the majority of the left side lower level of the left building. Samuel continued, "the abandoned quarters were in the process of being remodeled but they are currently in the planning stages, while the architects are planning there will be no one attending to this section of the temple. This space would be ideal for AY to hide a child away from anyone looking for her."

The plan would be to get on the caravan just before sunrise, travel to the kingdom, and then find the tunnel entrances to move through the tunnel corridors to the Queens old chambers, grab Raven and get back to the caravan before sunset to travel back home. The friends agreed they would do everything possible to blend in, remain undetected, and get out quickly.

Steven, the eternal voice of reason spoke up and said, "What if we get caught? What do we do, who do we call, what do we say? We can't say, oh we just came to take our sister who was kidnapped by an unknown servant for Vizier AY, but we just want to take her home now!"

Just as Steven finished his statement, he heard the hearty voice of his father behind him. Steven and Miriam both became stiff as a board like they were statutes hoping no one could see them. Tuhar entered the courtyard and simply said, "You will tell them you are on an assignment for Governor Tuhar and if there is a problem the guards are to bring the entire lot of you to me. You are also to tell them that the Governor has been in Conference with the King and this assignment was at his request."

Firesky, who was running only on adrenaline turned and barreled over to Governor Tuhar and wrapped his arms around him. Governor Tuhar was a large man and Firesky's arms could only reach around his sides. Apparently, Firesky's embrace did not surprise Governor Tuhar as he embraced Firesky back as if to share in their unspoken and un-displayed emotion for their missing Raven. Firesky released Governor Tuhar and Steven took Firesky's place and embraced his father. Tuhar knew his son was terrified but hugged him in a way that he was trying to transfer all of his courage to his son because he knew that Firesky needed his best friend on this journey.

It was only about two hours before the caravan would be leaving for the Kingdom, so Miriam and her Grandfather returned to their home to prepare for the trip. While Salihah and

Lateef sat with Firesky in their living room holding him like it would be their last time. Steven returned to his home with Imani and his parents to pack food and any supplies they might need for the trip.

The kids met the caravan that was made up of three traveling wagons, one designated for transporting the agriculture and trading products that would be sold on trader's row. The second wagon held the supplies needed to setup the display of the goods, while the third wagon was for the people traveling with the caravan. Firesky hugged his mom, who was visibly crying, and then his dad who gave him an assuring hug and kissed his son on the top of his head. Steven had his arms wrapped about the waists of both his mom and dad. As they arrived at the footstool of the third wagon that was being driven by Samuel, Imani stepped forward to each of the kids and put an amulet necklace on each and kissed them on their cheek. She whispered a prayer of covering and protection over their life and for a safe journey. Steven was the last to receive his amulet necklace and prayer and as Imani finished her prayer he grabbed and embraced her. Young Steven only ten years old held onto his now sixteen-year-old sister. Even with the six-year age gap Steven was almost as tall as his older sister. They embraced and Imani broke the contact, visibly crying to give Steven an assuring look to let him know he would return safely to her.

Aaron and Apollo were the first to board the caravan, both had extremely large backpacks, like they were expecting to be lost in the mountains of Sanai for months. Miriam boarded behind the twins and sat directly behind her grandfather, followed by Steven and finally Firesky. The children were the last to board the caravan and it took off toward the Nile just after the wagon gate closed. Firesky sat stoically in his seat and did not turn around to wave goodbye to his parents. He felt he was losing courage and one last look at his parents would make him break and not go to Egypt at all. The trip to the Nile would only last about twenty minutes as the loading docks to the traveling ferries were located at the north end of the city of Khuhua. The trip to trader's row would take about two hours, long enough for the kids to catch a nap before the true journey began.

The caravan wagons were the only travelers on the ferries this morning and as the sun crested the horizon the caravans were locked in on the ferry and they were underway along the Nile. As Firesky drifted off to sleep his last fleeting thought was of Aaron's lingering statement, just be ready for what happens after she is saved.

CHAPTER SEVENTEEN

GET ME A PRIEST

The loud horn on the ferry sounded and woke all of its travelers. They were riding into Egypt at the rear of the Temple of Tutankhamun. Along the Nile, Firesky could see several docking stations, at least five, in the rear of the temple. The massive structure looked like walls of bricks in multiple shades of brown. The walls were no less than three and a half meters tall with a structure of pillars on top of the walls. As the ferry moved closer to one of the docking stations, Firesky could see the landing ramps that would allow the wagons to easily bring their products to trader's row. The pillars that aligned the ramp were decorated with images of the towns that surrounded and supported Egypt, the harvests, the battles that had taken place in Egypt, the temples in north and south Egypt and other pictures

Firesky did not understand. The grandness of the temple made Firesky feel very small, and his fears started welling up. As he felt a warm wet tear hit his cheek, he looked up to see a young lady standing next to the last pillar at the top of the ramp. She had long flowing, wavy jet-black hair like Raven's. Although she had her back turned to the Nile, just seeing her hair seemed to give Firesky the courage he needed to rescue his sister. The wagon made it to the top of the ramp, and the young lady turned and faced the wagon. Firesky noticed that although she was at least ten years older than Raven, she looked nothing like Raven. Firesky chuckled to himself with the thought, if he had seen her face first he would still be terrified and lack the courage to rescue his sister.

The caravan stopped in front of trader's row. The children could see the priest temple and the stables for the livestock and could see at the end of trader's row another building that could have been for the military. As he looked around he noticed a lot of commotion and movement from the people both inside and out of trader's row. Just then three soldiers approached the driver of their caravan two wagons in front of them. The children leaned over the side of the wagon to see what the soldiers were doing. Aaron saw that the soldiers were looking in the bags of the caravan drivers for both the first and second wagon which had no other passengers. Aaron sat up in his seat looking away from the soldiers and tapped Apollo on his arm. Apollo looked up to Aaron, as Aaron motioned with his eyes at his backpack. Firesky noticed Aaron and looked away from the soldiers who were preparing to come to their wagon. Firesky mouthed silently to Aaron, what's wrong?

Aaron made motions toward his backpack, like charades, to indicate he had some items in his bag that the soldiers would not allow them to keep. Aaron made a motion where he had his fingertips all come together like he was attempting to grasp two sides of a string and pull them apart. Then he motioned like he was throwing something to the ground and when it hit he extended his fingers as if to demonstrate a billow of smoke or a loud sound. The beauty of being a group of ten and twelve-year-old kids was the ability to understand an unspoken language of charades very easily. Firesky understood that Aaron and Apollo had some tools that would likely be taken away if the soldiers were to inspect their bag. They had to think quickly before the soldiers arrived, and by this time both Miriam and Steven understood their journey could end before it started if the soldiers discovered what was in their backpacks.

The three soldiers were about three paces from reaching Samuel who was leading the third wagon when Miriam stood up and started crying. There were about twenty people on the wagon that all turned to look at Miriam who out of nowhere just started crying. Not only did Miriam start crying, but she also started screaming prayers. Everyone on the wagon started moving away from where Miriam stood in the center of the wagon, and the soldiers made their way over to the back of the wagon. One of the soldiers boarded the wagon in an attempt to calm Miriam down as she was now making a real scene. Samuel apparently understood what was going on and made no moves to console his granddaughter. The rest of the persons on the caravan got off of the caravan while Miriam continued to get louder with her crying and screaming prayers for the lost girl. Miriam was so inconsolable by the one soldier that the other soldiers came aboard to try to calm her down. They became part of the spectacle as they were screaming just as loud as she was trying to calm her down. Apollo, now safely off the wagon with his backpack in tow, had to turn around to keep the soldiers from seeing him start to laugh uncontrollably. Miriam made one last decree to the Gods to save her neighbor who was kidnapped and looked pointedly at one of the soldiers and screamed as loud as she could, "GET ME A PRIEST!"

The soldiers, who were visibly flustered by the situation, helped Miriam off of the wagon and took her to the priest temple trying to console her on the way. Miriam made the soldiers stop as she turned and motioned to her friends to come with her. She looked up to the soldiers and said with a tearful plea we are all from the town of the kidnapped girl, I think we all need to pray to the

Gods for her safe return. Miriam finished her plea with a loud, "PLEASE!"

The soldiers motioned to the kids to come along with them to the priest's temple. Apollo was now crying from having to hold in his laughter. One of the soldiers mistook his tears of laughter for sadness and came to his side to console him and escort him to the priest temple. When they reached the priest's temple, Miriam turned and surprised the soldiers with a hug and thanked him for understanding. As if her performance wasn't extreme enough, she topped it off by telling all three soldiers she would say a prayer for them as well. The soldiers stayed at the bottom of the stairs to watch the children ascend the stairs and enter the priest's temple.

As the children entered the temple, they all burst into fits of laughter and tried their best to be undetected by the temple priests. But they noticed there was activity going on in the temple that kept them from being noticed. Still teared up from laughing so hard they made their way forward to the auditorium of the priest temple which sat just beyond the foyer of the temple. As they approached the stairs which descended about five steps into the auditorium they saw what looked like hundreds of young girls. There were about thirty priests and priestesses that surrounded the group of girls who appeared to be there willingly. After about two minutes, Miriam felt a hand on her arm that ushered her down the stairs into the crowd of girls and told her to remove her head covering. Miriam was so stunned she made no moves to reject the advancing of whom she turned and saw was a priest.

Another priest approached the boys and guided them to a viewing area where there were about forty other men and boys watching from what looked like a viewing area of the auditorium. Steven noticed a young man standing to the right of the viewing window he knew. He had attended some of the state dinners his father Governor Tuhar would host in and out of Khuhua. Steven approached the young man who turned and recognized Steven as well. Steven asked about his family and then inquired about what was happening in the hall. The young man, named Gali, told Steven that this was the selection process of positioning young ladies in the kings and queens court. When a young girl of status from the local communities were eleven or twelve, they were brought to the priests for them to evaluate and select them for the queen's court. Those unselected as attendants for the courts could then be assigned to various positions in and around the kingdom. The young man went on to explain that it would be a great honor for these young ladies to be selected as it puts them in a position to be selected as a wife for a member of the military leadership or they may become a priestess. Gali continued his animated explanation while Aaron, Apollo, and Firesky joined them. Gali greeted each of them warmly, as he knew they were Steven's friends. Gali finished his explanation by telling the boys that the selection process was supposed to start earlier, but apparently a neighboring city had a girl kidnapped and the King ordered that every resource be used to search for the girl. The King believes the girl was kidnapped and brought here to the kingdom because it would be selection weekend and she could get lost in the sea of girls.

Gali added I don't think she is here because from the reports the girl is only 4 or 5 and it would be apparent that she would be too young for the selection process.

Without knowing it, Gali helped the boys know that Raven was not in the priest temple. Now they would need to get Miriam out of the sea of girls and on to the Queens abandoned quarters. Steven thanked Gali for the information, and he and the other boys retired to the rear of the viewing area. Firesky looked at Aaron and Apollo and asked what they could use in their backpack. Aaron had a sheepish look on his face; he obviously had an idea.

Aaron said, "you remember when we let the pig loose through the fields and pretended the ghost of a God had returned using the thing my dad created for hunting to make animal sounds? I say it's time to become an animal in the temple."

Apollo chuckled and added, "let's add the blanket."

Whatever the blanket meant, Firesky knew this was about to be just as dramatic as Miriam screaming and crying at the top of her lungs at the back of the wagon. Aaron and Apollo told Firesky and Steven they would handle everything, just be ready to grab Miriam to get out of the priest temple.

Firesky and Steven walked back to the front of the viewing window and began searching the sea of girls for Miriam. The girls were engaged in animated conversations with each other and moved around the floor. Finally, Steven spotted a single girl who was not talking to anyone but instead was staring up at the viewing window. Steven had to squint his eyes to make out Miriam who had let down her long dark brown hair that had streaks of light brown which would appear each year during the hot months. Because Miriam's family was from the Nubian nation her skin was a beautiful dark brown, she had long black eyelashes that framed her wide eyes, and dark brown almost black eyes which were pinched on their outer rim. Miriam was by far the most beautiful girl in the room, even with her boyish stature. When the two made eye contact, Steven motioned to her to move toward the entrance of the hall. Miriam did not hesitate to start moving that way.

Steven looked away from the hall and noticed that both Aaron and Apollo had disappeared from the room. He knew the twins were fearless and they would make their move soon. Out of nowhere, Steven heard the low sounds of a large cat sounding like it was just outside of the hall. Steven started chuckling to himself and made his way slowly toward the front of the hall with Firesky at his side. As quickly as he heard the sound, it went silent. He took a quick glance into the hall from the edge of the viewing window and saw the priests who were surrounding the girls looking suspiciously at each other as if they were checking with each other to see if anyone else heard the sounds. Then suddenly Steven saw the left side of the hall crowd of girls separate as a large sandy colored blanket begin to move from side to side as if an animal were trapped underneath. The sound of the cat started again and grew louder while the movement underneath the blanket grew more erratic as if the cat would emerge from the blanket and attack one of the girls, or worst yet, a priest. The sound of the cat grew even louder, and the priests, like the girls simply moved away from the movement of the blanket at what seemed to be a small animal making its way across the hall. The blanket covered animal made a single stop in the middle of the hall and made a slow complete circle as the animal sounds grew more territorial and vicious and then proceeded to make its way out of the front of the priest's temple. Steven and Firesky giggling made their way to the front of the priest's temple, and no one noticed that Miriam too had made her way out of the front door.

Aaron stood at the left of the front door increasing his animal sounds like the cat was attacking and then started moving away from the door to make it sound as if the animal had made its way from the priest's temple. Since all of the priests had been inside for the selection process, there were no straggling priests outside to catch the children in their acts of mischief. They were surprised that all of the soldiers seemed to be preoccupied with running around the kingdom, presumably focused on finding Raven. The kids had no time to revel in the excitement of escaping the priest temple, time was passing, and they had not found Raven to make sure they got out in time to make it back to the caravan. Aaron and Apollo repacked the blanket and their hunting gear, while Miriam rewrapped her hair and they laughed their way back to trader's row to check in with Samuel and give him a status update.

As they approached Samuel, the children become sober as the look on Samuels face told them something was wrong. Samuel informed them that Traders Row would be canceled this day, by order of King Tutankhamun. He was concerned that the crowds would give an opportunity for the person who took the child to move her around or to another location without being detected. We have been ordered not to unpack our goods, and we would be told to leave as soon as they had inspected everyone's belongings. I could stall the departure because the ferry had already left the port and would not return until the evening. However, if the soldiers offer another ferry to take the group to Khuhua I would not be able to stop the departure. You all need to hurry and find the child.

Steven, who was ordinarily too afraid to try anything different, told the group, "let me talk to the king."

Firesky responded to his friend, "Let us talk to the king!"

Both Miriam and Apollo looked at their friends with a look of concern, Miriam responded, "Are you sure? You know he could kill you both for coming into his presence without his permission. And also, let's not mention that AY could be anywhere, just waiting to capture and kill you for knowing it could have potentially been him that ordered Raven's kidnapping."

Steven looked over to Miriam and asked, "Do you have a better idea?"

Neither Miriam or anyone else had a better

idea, and responded, "Ok, let's go!"

Both Steven and Firesky, responded together, "No! just us." Steven pointed to Firesky and then to himself.

Aaron and Apollo, said, "I don't think that is a good idea, but I have an idea that might help. Our brother is working in the temple today if we can find him he can help us get to the Queens abandoned quarters while you and Firesky get to the King. If we get to Raven first, we would bring her back to Samuel, wrap her in disguise and load her on the wagon. You guys just make sure you get back in time to get on the caravan and the ferry before it leaves."

None of them were completely comfortable with this plan, but short of having another idea, this was the best they could do. Aaron and Apollo could use Miriam to safely get in and out of the Queens quarters with Raven, if she were surrounded by attendants. Also, if Steven and Firesky could reach King Tutankhamun to convince him to let trader's row happen for the day, they would all have more time, and the king would be in on the plan.

Before the kids departed, Samuel grabbed the arms of both Firesky and Steven. "I have some sashes for each of you. When I was the chief architect, I had free reign to move about the temples because I always had these sashes. The sashes identified me as a member of leadership as appointed by the king. When King Tutankhamun came to Khuhua the last time I wore my sash on my right arm, and he saluted me and thanked me for my service. You see, once a leader in the king's court, as long as you have not committed a crime, you are always recognized as a leader in the court. If you have these on your arms, as I have already given Miriam from her mother, you will always be permitted to have an audience with the Kings leadership."

Steven, glanced at Miriam and whispered, "Your mother was a member of the Kings leadership?'

Miriam gave Steven a weak smile and told

him, "When you return safely I will tell you all about it."

Steven nodded, and both he and Firesky thanked Samuel, turned and walked toward the front of the Temple of Tutankhamun. As they walked, they examined the sashes on their arms thankful for taking this journey with Samuel and all of their friends. Meanwhile, Samuel gave guidance to Miriam, Aaron, and Apollo regarding where they could go to get into the inside tunnels to find and rescue Raven. From where the children were standing Samuel showed them a marking on the wall of the building that was about 9 meters away. Samuel told them, everywhere they saw that mark that looked like a four-headed snake underneath it would be a doorway to the inside tunnels, and they would be able to navigate their way through the corridors. Their current position was the west building, and they would need to get to the rear of the east building of the temple. Samuel kissed Miriam on the forehead and wish the trio good luck.

Miriam took the first steps toward the

inside tunnels and just before reaching the doors a soldier called out to them to stop. The soldier who instructed them to stop was standing behind them, and the terrified children slowly turned to face the soldier. As Apollo turned, he was reaching for a shock bomb, which was a small toy that when thrown to the ground put up a puff of smoke and made a loud sound. The smoke and loud sound would throw off their attackers long enough for them to get away. The shock bomb worked in the past for the twins on both animals and humans. As they completed their turn and came face to face with the soldier, Miriam discovered that it was one of the soldiers who had attempted to console her on the wagon. Although the kids had failed to take a breath once the soldier requested they stop, Miriam was able to gather herself and smile at the soldier.

The soldier stated, "Miss, are you alright now? We were all very concerned about you."

Miriam quickly teared up, and reassured the soldier, "it still upsets me to think about the lost girl, but the Gods have assured me she will be safely returned to her family." Miriam asked the soldier, "Have you found her yet?"

The soldier replied, "Unfortunately, we have not, but our King has tripled the number of soldiers looking for the child." The soldier then retorted, "you would think the child was his child." Apparently, the soldier internally scolded himself because he immediately apologized to the children saying, "children are a blessing, and I should respect that any child missing is a tragedy." The soldier recovered himself and rubbed the arm of Miriam, showing that he was happy she felt better. The soldier then left the children heading for the priest's temple.

The children turned back to the wall, with a quick glance to see if anyone else was watching them, opened the door and entered the inside tunnel. The tunnels were dark with minimal light but surprisingly dry. Aaron took the lamp he had the previous night from his backpack and lit it up for their journey. Aaron and Apollo had previously been in the tunnels, although they weren't aware at the time the tunnels flowed throughout the Kingdom. They had been there with their brother once before because of his job. Apollo remembered that there were signs and symbols along the walls that would tell them how to get from one place to another within the corridors. On the walls were directional signs, one just needed to know to read them. Soon after beginning their search they found the symbols for the baker's shop and made their way to find Aaron and Apollos older brother.

CHAPTER EIGHTEEN

WOULD YOU BE WILLING

Steven and Firesky took the first steps toward the temple and were confronted by the Kings Guards. The guards, who looked foreboding, asked the two boys,

" What are you doing here?"

Steven could not speak, he was paralyzed by fear. The only thing he could think to do was to show the guards the sash on his right arm. The guards look at each other, confused about what to do next.

Firesky, recognizing the confusion on their faces, told the guards," We are here on official assignment from the Governor of Khuhua, Governor Tuhar. He has sent us to request an audience with King Tutankhamun."

The guards had never been confronted with such a request from children, and they were very unsure about what to do. The children were here in some official capacity as they knew the name of the Governor of Tuhar and they wore the sashes of official Egyptian leadership. Just as it appeared they were going to let the boys enter the temple; Commander Horemheb appeared flanked by no less than twenty other soldiers. The Commander was a large man who towered over Firesky even greater than his father. He was a dark-skinned man with a round unfriendly face. To the boys, he was likely the most intimidating figure they had ever seen.

Commander Horemheb asked the soldier to escort the boys to his office, and he would be there shortly. As Steven and Firesky made their way with their escorts to Commander Horemheb's office which was not in the main temple, but rather the building they saw from trader's row. They caught a piece of what Commander Horemheb was saying to his soldier,

"Do not inform AY." The boy's escorts were moving double time, and the boys had to move with haste; almost to a run to keep up. They made it to Commander Horemheb 's office which was the first office to the right of the inside foyer of the military building.

Commander Horemheb seemed to be running to his office, as he stepped into his office in what seemed like moments after the boys arrived and took their seats. Commander Horemheb, almost looked relieved to see the boys and wasted no time telling them his intentions.

"We will have a visitor shortly, but I need you boys to tell me what you are doing here at the Kingdom and how you came to have those sashes," the Commander said in haste.

Firesky responded, "Sir we are here on assignment from Governor Tuhar to speak to King Tutankhamun about an urgent matter…"

Commander Horemheb interrupted Firesky to ask, "Are you here about the girl?"

Firesky, surprised by Commander Horemheb statement, responded with a question instead of an answer, "What do you know about the girl?"

Commander Horemheb flashed a rare and friendly smile, "You are here about the girl! Please tell me what you know!"

"Sir, she is my sister and my family, and I want her back. My only job was to protect her, and I failed to do so. So, I am here searching for her so I can take her home. That means everything to me," Firesky responded fighting off the urge to cry.

Commander Horemheb's facial expression softened as if he was relieved to hear Firesky's response. Commander Horemheb took a few moments to respond and said, "Well, that changes things!"

His response seemed odd to the boys, and they suspected he wanted to clarify if Raven was King Tutankhamun's child. Firesky's response seemed to clear it up for him because his follow-up shocked them.

Commander Horemheb asked the boys, "How can I help you?"

This mission seemed to have just gotten a lot easier, they hoped. "Commander Horemheb, we need to speak with King Tutankhamun and fast," Firesky responded.

Just as Firesky finished his request, the door to Commander Horemheb's office began to jiggle to suggest someone was entering the room. The door seemed to move in slow motion, and the first thing Firesky saw as he watched the door was the bright gold chest plate of King Tutankhamun. As King Tutankhamun opened the door fully, the boys could see he was engaged in a heated discussion with another person just beyond the threshold of Commander Horemheb's office. The Commander stood to his feet out of respect for the king and the boys followed suite as they saw King Tutankhamun enter the room followed by his vizier AY. The two were discussing the search for the girl, as King Tutankhamun was angrily expressing to AY that the search would continue and AY was saying there were other important things to do rather than search for a girl who may or may not be in the kingdom.

As King Tutankhamun crossed the threshold into Commander Horemheb's office, who was also shocked to see AY in conversation with King Tutankhamun, he immediately recognized the boys in the corner seats in the office. He immediately ceased his conversation with AY to address the boys who were completely speechless. King Tutankhamun nodded at Commander Horemheb to acknowledge his presence and also to respect his office and position. King Tutankhamun then walked over to the boys who were standing and glaring past the king at AY with an intense anger King Tutankhamun had never seen from the boys. Although King Tutankhamun recognized the look, he ignored their disdain and asked them about their purpose for being in Egypt.

Before King Tutankhamun would allow the boys to speak, he told Firesky, "I am so sorry about your sister, I know Lateef and Salihah must be overwhelmed with grief. I am trying to fulfill my commitment to them that I would do anything to help find the child. If she is in Egypt, we will find her."

Firesky was so confused at that moment; he didn't know what to do or say. He simply stared at King Tutankhamun with a look of bewilderment. Steven found his voice and thanked the king for helping his friend and their family. Finally, after Steven finished, Firesky responded, "We came over today to help with trader's row, but we hear you have canceled it for today. Would it be possible to let it happen today, as we wanted to work to get our minds off of the grief of the situation?"

Firesky was diligently trying to communicate with King Tutankhamun, hoping he would grasp what he was not saying to him. He needed the additional time for him and his friends to find Raven. He needed to make sure the caravan did not leave them before they could save her and get back home.

Steven noticed that AY was glaring at the boys, searching their faces for a clue as to whether or not they knew he was involved. Apparently, at that moment Steven garnished more courage than Firesky had ever seen from his best friend. Firesky didn't know if it was because of his anger or his sheer hatred for this man, but he saw his friend muster the courage to address AY directly.

Steven asked AY, "Would you be willing to help us find our beloved daughter of Khuhua? Would you be willing to make sure she is found alive and safe and sound? I know you have hated my family, but this is the daughter of everyone in our city and we desperately want her back, can you help us?"

Steven began to take a step towards AY, and pass by King Tutankhamun when Tutankhamun grabbed Steven into a one-armed bear hug. With his right hand on his cane,

Tutankhamun grabbed Steven around his shoulders and pulled him into his chest. The King knew Steven would soon become so overwhelmed with emotion that he would not be able to control his words or actions. The only way King Tutankhamun could break the tension was to embrace Steven and allow his emotions to be released through his tears into the Kings chest instead of through his words that were escalating to an outright accusation at AY for kidnapping Raven.

As King Tutankhamun consoled a very emotional Steven, AY finally found his voice and responded to Steven's request, "Yes, of course, I will help you find her. If the child is here, we will find her."

King Tutankhamun either felt the angry heat rising from Firesky or noticed his body language that showed, like Steven, Firesky was about to blow. King Tutankhamun steadied himself, laid his cane on Commander Horemheb's desk and pulled Firesky into a hug as well. Commander Horemheb came to King

Tutankhamun's aid and grabbed Steven from King Tutankhamun to console the boy.

AY, who was visibly uncomfortable began to turn to leave the office, when King Tutankhamun asked him to stay and strategize with Commander Horemheb how we are going to allow Trader's row to take place on this day while simultaneously using every resource they have to find the girl and return her to her family. The king followed up and told both AY and Commander Horemheb, "The Kingdom has made a promise to their ally, and we will do everything possible to find the girl and return her to her family. I will take the boys with me."

King Tutankhamun looked both Steven and Firesky in their tear-filled eyes and said, "Continue walking in your destiny, no matter what it looks like!"

Both Steven and Firesky understood what King Tutankhamun was referring too, the message he gave them before Raven's kidnapping. Both boys physically calmed down from the excitement in

Commander Horemheb's office. As they made haste with King Tutankhamun back to his temple, Tutankhamun whispered, "I heard your message loud and clear, now let's go get our girl."

CHAPTER NINETEEN

LIGHT THEM UP

Aaron and Apollo with Miriam found their brother in the baker's shop, and he already knew about Raven's kidnapping. He was also aware of where Raven could have been. Because of his position, he could not participate in finding her but would be able to tell them exactly how to find her and avoid the challenge of traveling from corridor to corridor within the inside tunnels. As the trio made their way through the tunnels, they were distracted by the various conversations going on beyond the walls. At one point Aaron stopped to hear an exchange between two people arguing over salt. The three stopped long enough to hear the conversation, start laughing, and realized they could be heard through the walls, as the two-people stopped arguing when they heard the laughter in the walls. The children quickly moved through the tunnels to the east wing to where the Queens original chambers were.

The trio grew closer and heard several voices through the wall, as they stopped to hear the conversation they recognized there were two individuals in a heated discussion. The two individuals were discussing the punishment for getting caught kidnapping a child. The male voice sounded very upset and could have been crying as he said, "I am going to be put to death in the most horrendous way. They will spare no level of torture once they catch me for this crime. Why did I take the money? There is no amount of money that could save my life?"

The female voice interrupted and stated, "I thought you did this for your child, your money will help him have a better future. This was never about you if you die you will die with honor."

The male voice followed by saying, "This is stupid if I just disappear no one will ever know it was me. We should just go."

From behind the wall Aaron, Apollo, and Miriam were not sure what to do. They did not hear Raven's voice in the room. If they interrupted them now and Raven was not in the room, then what, they would leave empty-handed. Over the next few moments, the trio discussed what to do, considering while they were in the corridor's they would have no idea what time it was and the caravan could have already left them stuck in Egypt.

Finally, Miriam heard the voice of Raven enter the room. She was being classic Raven, asking whoever was ushering her into the room a battery of questions.

"My mommy is so pretty, but she doesn't have hair like mine, hers is brown and shorter than my hair, do you have a mommy? Mommy's are so great; I miss my mommy. I thought you said my Mommy and Daddy were coming to visit me. Did you tell me a lie? You know lies are really, really bad! I get in trouble every time I tell a lie, even if it is a small lie I tell my brother when we are playing. I have the best brother in the world. You know sometimes I mess with him, because I know he is supposed to watch me, and I disappear when he is playing so he will come and find me. We play on the river sometimes, even though my mommy and daddy don't like us to. Did you know there are Crocodiles in the Nile, they come to eat little girls like me..." Raven was on a roll telling whomever she was talking to everything that was on her mind.

Aaron, Apollo, and Miriam all chuckled to themselves quietly, so as not to get discovered, by the persons on the other side of the door. Miriam whispered to Aaron and Apollo; they will be so happy to be rescued from Raven.

Aaron responded saying, "I bet they didn't know what they signed up for, "while they all continued to laugh.

Knowing they were running out of time Aaron looked at Apollo and asked," Vanishing Act?"

Apollo nodded and then said in a loud

whisper, "LIGHT THEM UP!"

Aaron reached into his backpack, pulled out a handful of smoke bombs and a second handful for Ravens colors, as the combination of the smoke bombs and colors that Aaron and Apollos dad had created for Raven would make the smoke appear in a variety of colors.

Miriam held the door handle and waited for Aaron's signal, as they continued to hear the battery of questions Raven continued to throw at her attendees. Aaron put three smoke bombs in his pocket and then combined the rest of the smoke bombs and colors into one hand. Miriam opened the door and Aaron threw the smoke bombs in the room as hard as he could. In five seconds the room was filled with billows of colorful smoke and loud noises and all Aaron, Apollo, and Miriam could hear were screams and footsteps running away from the room. When the shots died down, Miriam called out to Raven who had taken a seat on the ground waiting for her rescuers. As the smoke cleared, the trio could see Raven sitting on the floor laughing and playing with the colorful smoke. So many times before she had seen Aaron and Apollo do that trick and she would be filled with fits of laughter.

Miriam walked up to Raven and asked, "Are you ready to go?"

Raven, looking reluctant, asked, "Where's my brother, I just knew he was coming to get me."

Miriam looked at Aaron and Apollo, who were smiling, then back at Raven and answered, "Firesky will be waiting for you outside. Let's go."

In classic Raven style, she started with the questions, "Are we going home? I am ready to go home! Did you know they did not like my hair! I think they were lying; they liked my hair. Do you like my hair?"

Miriam answered, "Raven I think your hair is beautiful and I think they were lying too! Yes, let's go home."

With Raven in tow, the trio guided Raven through the tunnels and explained that during this time she would have to be very quiet so that no one came to take her again. Somehow that was enough to get the most talkative girl they knew to be quiet.

As they walked through the tunnels they approached a room with voices they recognized; it was Firesky and Steven. They seemed to be in a conversation with a third voice that sounded familiar, but they could not place.

Raven, recognized the voice and yelled," it's the King!"

On the other of side the wall the voices hushed, as Miriam opened the door from the corridor. They found Firesky, Steven, and King Tutankhamun looking at architectural plans of the temple. Once the door was opened, Raven ran straight into the arms of Firesky who burst into tears upon seeing his sister. All of the anxiety, fear, and stress he was experiencing, along with all of the thoughts of what could have happened to Raven came to the surface, and all he could do was weep with her in his arms. Raven leaned back to look at Firesky in the face and told him, "don't cry I am sorry if I made you worry, but I have a lot to tell you."

Firesky started laughing through his tears, because he was certain she would tell him everything in great detail. He then told Raven, "I want to hear everything!"

Raven turned to King Tutankhamun, who was also teary-eyed, and ran into his arms. He was so happy to hold his baby girl, no matter the circumstances this was his little girl whom he loved more than Egypt and more than his own life. This was the gift of his life, and he wished he could hold her forever. The King looked out of the library window and noticed the sun was on its way down.

"We have to get you back to the caravan, now!" said King Tutankhamun.

"Thank you for everything," Steven

responded

Firesky, who wanted to savor the moment, had to ask, "is it over? Do we still need to fear that AY will keep trying to kill Raven?

King Tutankhamun wanted to give Firesky and the others a more reassuring look, but they all grasped the gravity of the situation, it was not over, and the King would not always be there to keep Raven safe. King Tutankhamun promised he would do what he could but it was time to garner a new plan with the community that would make everyone in the community safer and protect the future of this beautiful soul, he put his hand under her chin leaned down and kissed Raven on the cheek.

He followed the kiss with a message in her ear, "You deserve the World, and I am going to do all I can to give it to you!"

Raven turned to King Tutankhamun, wrapped her arms around his neck and kissed him back then whispered in his ear, "I Love You, my

King."

At that moment King Tutankhamun was made whole. No matter what happened next in his life, he had the perfect moment.

CHAPTER TWENTY

PLEASE DON'T PRETEND

The children made it to the caravan by the skin of their teeth, using the corridors to come out at the same spot they had entered at the beginning of trader's row. Samuel spotted them running down the landing ramp toward the wagon which was next in line to board the ferry for Khuhua. He smiled knowing they made it safely and in time, but also because he saw the sweet face of Raven along with the children. This would be a great night for Khuhua.

The children boarded the wagon followed by its boarding onto the ferry. Raven sat in Firesky's lap the entire ride home and fell asleep shortly after leaving the Temple of Tutankhamun. As Raven fell off to sleep, Steven burst into a fit of uncontrollable laughter, trying with great difficulty to explain that the funniest thing he had ever seen was Apollo underneath the sand color blanket moving like a cat to Aaron cat sounds. Once they all got out of Steven what he was laughing about, they all fell into a fit of laughter and then fell into a restful sleep the rest of the way home.

They were all awakened by the horn of the ferry announcing its intention to dock at the port of Khuhua. Awakened by the horn, Firesky took the time to adjust his eyes to the dim light on the ferry moving closer to the lights on the dock at Khuhua. He saw a crowd of people standing on the dock, more than usual when a ferry comes in. Firesky made out his mother and father, the Governor and his wife, even Aaron and Apollos mom was at the dock. Behind them seemed like the entire community of Khuhua who were all waiting with baited breath to see if their daughter had returned home.

The Ferry made its turn to back into the dock, and Raven lifted her head from Firesky's arm. The glimpse of Raven was met with great cheers and hugs to each other in the community. As Raven heard the cheers, she stood, using Firesky to brace her and gave a big wave to everyone at the dock who clapped and cheered louder than before. The ferry docked, and everyone made sure to let Raven be the first one off the boat.

Raven ran straight into Salihah arms, who was already weeping from joy to see her baby girl and boy both return home safe and sound. Lateef wrapped Raven and her mom into a bear hug and then grabbed Firesky when he finally made it off the dock to them. The sounds of relief were heard throughout the entire community.

Imani, who was so overcome with emotion had to sit on the ground holding her head in her face and cry. After a few moments, she felt the small hand of Raven on her head, she lifted her tear stained face and wrapped Raven into her arms so hard Raven fell into her lap. Raven told her she got to kiss the King and tell him she loved him. At Raven's confession, Imani wept harder and held her closer. Firesky came to Imani's side, and she pulled him down with them and just hugged and loved on the two of them. When Aaron, Apollo, Miriam, and Steven saw them on the ground, they all ran and joined in on the ground hug while everyone in the community laughed a necessary therapeutic laugh.

The celebration ended late into the evening, but finally, everyone made it safely to their bed for much-needed rest. The next morning it appeared the city of Khuhua was finally able to return to its normal schedule of business, but to no avail. While Governor Khuhua and the local governing body were meeting in the main square, there was a commotion of horses and people outside of the building. Governor Tuhar made his way outside flanked by other local leaders to see AY in the middle of the square with his band of military officials, including Commander Horemheb along with two individuals who appeared to have been beaten to within an inch of their lives. He had several soldiers readied with Axes to decapitate the two individuals. When Tuhar reached the square with his wife and other leaders at his side, he yelled to AY, "WHAT

ARE YOU DOING HERE, WHAT IS THIS
SPECTACLE?"

AY responded, "these are the kidnappers
who took the daughter of Khuhua who will pay
for their crimes with their lives."

AY did not await Tuhar response, and
instead dropped his hand, and in response, the
soldiers dropped the axes on the necks of the two
suspected criminals and killed them. Tuhar,
feeling disgusted by the actions of AY, knowing
the criminals did not act without his express
guidance turned and returned to his office. He
asked one of the local officials to tell AY he was
responsible for cleaning up the mess and getting
that spectacle out of his city.

AY, who felt Tuhar disrespected him
decided to confront Tuhar in his office. He
ordered his soldiers to clean up the bodies and the
square and then made his way to the meeting of
the local officials of Khuhua. The appearance of
AY in Tuhar's office infuriated Tuhar and had his
wife not grabbed his arm he would likely have

thrown AY out of the top floor window of his building. Instead, he guided AY to his private office.

Tuhar only allowed AY to cross the threshold of his office before he confronted him, "Please don't pretend we all don't know this was a poor attempt to cover up your actions. We know you ordered Ravens kidnapping because you fear she is King Tutankhamun's child and yet again, as in the days of Amenhotep III and Akhenaten you will lose your opportunity to rule Egypt. I remember how you arrived in your position; I remember how you had to beg Akhenaten to give you a chance because of your daughter Nefertiti, I remember who you really are. You leave my office, my City, and our lives; I have no reason or use for you!"

AY glared at Tuhar but refrained from speaking, as everything he said was both accurate and painful. AY would take time to plan his revenge and the next time he would complete the job; and would end the possibility of losing his opportunity to rule over Egypt. He knew it would be just a matter of time before King Tutankhamun would be gone if he had to kill him, himself. There was no way he would ever let this child rule over Egypt, not while he was alive.

It was good that AY was in Khuhua, as David had returned to the temple with news from Amarna. He arrived at the temple just before noon the day after Raven had returned home. He immediately requested an audience with King Tutankhamun, who was still reeling from Raven's kiss and declaration of love. When Tutankhamun saw his friend, he made haste to embrace him, but as he came closer to him, he saw trepidation on this face.

"What is wrong my friend," Tutankhamun asked with great concern.

David replied, "You need to journey to Amarna with me, he means to start a war and destroy any memory of you, including Raven and Imani.

CHAPTER TWENTY-ONE

COME BACK TOMORROW

Aaron closed the book he had been reading the past four hours. While Aaron read the incredible story of Firesky and Raven I listened in disbelief, then took the time to follow the story while examining the drawings on the walls. I stared at the gold box drawing on the wall. Touching the walls felt like sandy concrete. Like feeling the sidewalks during the summertime in Fifty Lakes, after the local girls drew hopscotches and other drawings with chalk.

The gritty walls depicted the meeting between King Tutankhamun and Imani. It showed a younger King Tutankhamun, not as young as the boy king who became Pharaoh at eight years old, but a young man with poise and dignity standing atop the construction of the tunnels leading to each village with which the tunnels were built. The walls depicted the Ethiopian battle with Egypt. There was also an area that showcased the children who saved the little raven-haired girl, Firesky, Steven, Aaron, Apollo, and Miriam. There appeared on the wall a child who was ascending to the Gods, who I assumed was the child who died when Raven was born. As I followed the story on the walls, I noticed a picture of the same children atop a mountain holding a stone together and it appeared to be shining a light over the head of King Tutankhamun.

I turned and looked at Aaron, who again seemed to be watching my journey of exploration in the room. Aaron put the notebook he had been reading from into his backpack along with the Gold box and walked over to me at the back wall of the room behind the benches we sat on when Aaron began telling us the story. Aaron explained that there was so much more to tell me about Firesky's journey because it did not end when Raven came home. Instead, each of the children had to be pushed to their limits, they had to

THE JOURNEY CONTINUES...

ACKNOWLEDGEMENTS

To all who endured the endless hours of short-walk talks listening to the abundance of creativity within me. If you have had the chance to hear my stories, consider yourself blessed, and only you will understand what I mean. To my family who have supported me and always told me there are no limits. To my Great Grandmother, who I have never met but hope I have made you proud because I am pursuing my dream of writing and I stand on your shoulders. There are so many more stories to tell, to my fellow storytellers, reach for the skies.

To my Grandparents, on both sides of me, thank you for your love, your time, your encouragement, and endowing me with your gifts. To my Mom and Dad, you allow me to live in a world where I get to use my superpowers every day. To my brother and my sisters, you love and accept me just the way I am and I appreciate that.

To my teachers who never treated me differently and at the same time embraced my differences. Great teachers are a gift and I have had several, so I thank you so much.

A special thank you to my mom who never stopped giving me your all, there are not enough words to tell you how much I will forever honor your gifts to me.

ABOUT THE AUTHOR

Xavier is the CEO of Savior Publishing and the author of the wildly successful book series: The Adventures of Firesky. He is 13 years old and passionate about creating great stories, showcasing his superpower Autism, Lego's, and being his authentic self.

A storyteller in his heart, Xavier would go on short walks with members of his family and always have a new story to tell with incredible detail starting from the age of four. Stories are in his heart and seeks to use his life to share them with the world.

Lightning Source UK Ltd.
Milton Keynes UK
UKHW012352270519
343433UK00001B/4/P

9 780986 154218